I0621280

OTHER PEOPLE'S PROBLEMS

OTHER PEOPLE'S PROBLEMS

K. J. McCALL

JJ Publishers, LLC

Published by
JJ Publishers, LLC

11445 Weatherstone Dr.
Waynesboro, Pa. 17268

www.KJMcCall.com

Printed in the United States of America

Cover by Rick Holland, myvisionpress.com

Library of Congress Control Number: 2021915784

ISBN: 978-1-7375553-4-6

One

Grace Dawson   June, 1953

If I hadn't spent the summer of 1953 in Roanoke, Virginia working for Piedmont Investigations, there'd be nothing to write here and you'd be off reading somebody else's words. I would have passed the time in my hometown of Betula, helping my mother can quarts of green beans and missing my boyfriend, Obie, who had canned me last spring. As it happened, though, on the first day of my summer job, the first hour, I got a look at a genuine blackmail note and knew I'd have plenty to pen on the matter.

It was the third Saturday in June when I packed up and said goodbye to my roommate, Penny Thayer, the future as unknown to me then as outer space. Only a twenty-minute drive from Stapleton to Roanoke—such a short journey considering how far it took me in life. You might say the whole trip was free of setbacks. I found Piedmont Investigations at 722 Ivy Street, parked my car out front, Ray Driscoll met me in the deserted lobby and that was it.

He led me down a hall wallpapered in tan, stuck his head in somebody's office and said, "She's here, we'll be down in a while." In his office he waved me to a chair at a table and took the opposite chair himself.

Let me tell you a bit about Driscoll. He's a serious guy with no wedding ring, dark hair graying at the temples. It's got to be premature gray, though, because I wouldn't put him too much older than twenty-five or twenty-six. Can't say he's especially handsome, but there's something attractive about him.

And he's never one to waste time on small talk. I mean, he started right off saying, "Grace, before we discuss the details of the job, I want you to read this." Then he unfolded the blackmail note and handed it to me without further words. It was handwritten on lined paper and came out of an envelope with no return address.

Dear Robert,
  I know the secret you have been keeping from your wife and everyone else. I don't know you personally and I didn't go out of my way to find out. I stumbled onto your little misadventure quite by accident and I'm betting nobody else knows.
  When people do this sort of thing they must realize the risk. I'm your risk. Lucky for you it was me who found out because I'm ready to forget all about it and let you live your life. But, as with all things, there is a price.
  Simply mail $200 in cash to P.O. Box 45, Salem, Virginia. Wrap the cash in a piece of paper with your name on it. You'll be paying good money for my silence and that will be the end of it, nothing more than a business transaction.
  But, ignore this letter and I'll send the damning details to your wife and neighbors. Imagine how they will react.
  Robert, it's up to you.

"Who's Robert?" I asked evenly, as though such letters are commonplace in my world and no big deal, when it actually caused immediate goosebumps, tingling on the forehead and other familiar signs of alarm—signs I'd labeled the "prickly willys" when I was a kid.

"Bobby Miller. He's another investigator here. We passed his office." Driscoll folded the note and put it in the envelope.

"What'd he do?"

"Why do you assume he did anything? Could be a bluff."

"Could it?"

"Sure, it could. The sender might have mailed a dozen or more of these things hoping to hit on somebody with a guilty conscience."

"Oh, I hadn't thought of that."

"I might as well tell you, though, that Bobby *did* do something. Cheated on his wife last winter. She never found out and he wants to keep it that way. You'll meet him in a little while. I think you'll like him. He's a regular guy, a friend of mine for years, so I hope you won't hold his little indiscretion against him."

I didn't say anything but cheating on one's wife is not a little indiscretion, not to me. My father cheated on my mother. Now, just so you know, I dearly love my dad. But his philandering caused their divorce and, twenty years later, she's still bitter about it. And another thing: There's a definite possibility that Obie cheated on me. I know, I know. It's not the same thing, since we weren't married or even engaged, but we had a plan that I called official, so it's the next worst thing. What is it with men? Are they all like that?

"I still think it's a bluff," Driscoll went on, "but he's worried to distraction. I need to prove it for his sake if nothing else."

"How you gonna do that?"

3

"Well, that's where you come in. I arranged a summer job for you at the Salem Post Office, filling in for a woman who broke her wrist."

"I'm working at a post office this summer?" Didn't sound quite as exciting as the undercover job I had imagined.

"Yes, starting Monday, which is why we're meeting today. You'll go in as a regular employee, learn to weigh packages and sort mail, that type thing." He paused and tilted his head. "You look disappointed. Think it sounds dull?"

"Well …"

"In any undercover assignment, you're an actor playing a part. The real job, however, will always be about information. In this case, observe whether any letters come in for box 45, and find out who rented it. I'm guessing it won't be dull at all, not with the stealthy sneaking around it might require."

"Oh."

"You'll be gathering useful information, Grace. If other mail comes in, maybe Bobby's letter was not the only one, which would mean it's a fake and the sender doesn't know anything about his little misadventure. Either way, the guy probably broke a dozen laws when he decided to blackmail people and do it through the United States Post Office."

"Then, what will you do? Turn him over to the police?" This was beginning to sound good.

"Yes, definitely. But if it's really blackmail … eh … how and when we turn him over will be up to Bobby. Anyway, you'll get your post office paycheck in addition to the small salary from us. Should be enough to get you by."

"Two paychecks?"

"How about that, a little bonus."

"I just hope I'm worth the money. There's something safe about working for nothing."

4

"I think you'll do fine. That's why you're here."

"Thanks. What does it take to be good at this sort of thing?"

"That's easy to answer. It takes nerve and curiosity. And if they were the currency instead of dollars, we'd all be filthy rich." Driscoll grabbed the envelope and stood. "Come on, I'll introduce you to Bobby." On the way up the hall he pointed through a door. "This office belongs to Eleanor Penn, our office manager. We have five investigators, not counting the boss, and she takes care of us all."

"The boss?"

"Don't worry about him, he's rarely in town. You'll only be dealing with Bobby and me."

When I met Bobby Miller, he came around to the front of his desk, polite-like, to shake my hand as if I were somebody important. Blond hair dipping down in a wave, a good-looking man. "Are you willing to be our post office spy, Miss Dawson?" he asked, glancing at me, Driscoll, and back at me.

I nodded vigorously. "Please, call me Grace."

"Good. We like first names around here. Sorry to meet under these circumstances. You must think I'm a cad."

"No, not at all," I said, trying to mean it.

The three of us took chairs at an oblong table. Driscoll pulled out the envelope, waved it in the air and set it down in the center. "This guy is smart. Two hundred dollars is a lot of money. Most people could pay their rent three or four months with that amount. But it's not a fortune. Most could scrape it together if they had to."

Bobby seemed to stare at me and everything except the envelope, nervously clicking a matchbook cover against his front teeth.

"But, like I already said, I think it's a bluff. For one thing, nobody calls you Robert, not that I've ever heard."

"Only my Aunt Ida," Bobby said with the first hint of a smile.

"And the letter is awfully vague, don't you think? Could fit any manner of crime. Burglary, assault, hit and run, lying under oath, embezzlement, counterfeit. Even murder."

"I guess you're right. It could." Bobby nodded several times, wanting to be convinced.

Driscoll tapped the envelope. "If he were targeting only you, surely he'd have been more specific, more threatening."

"Is it too early for me to say something?" I asked.

They both answered, "Of course not," at the same time.

"If you were this person, would you pick on an investigator? Dumb move, if you ask me. It would be like stealing a cop's automobile or breaking into his house. You just wouldn't do it if you knew." The two men raised eyebrows at each other. Their reaction spurred me on. "So, I'm guessing this guy doesn't know who you are or anything about you, including your misadventure. Probably just got your name out of the telephone book."

"Grace, that's perceptive. Don't you think so, Bobby?"

"Certainly is, and when it comes to believing this is a bluff, it's the most convincing argument yet." Bobby reached back to the corner of his desk, grabbed a small box and passed it to me. "This is a camera, Grace, one of the tools of the trade."

I opened it and removed what looked like a long cigarette lighter. It fit in my hand. "This is a camera?"

"It's a Minox, invented by a German, ironically enough. See how tiny it is? You can hide it in your pocket. They're essential to the spy game these days, used in all that skulking around the government has been doing with the Soviets."

6

"You can take a decent picture with this thing?"

"Sure, you can. The film canister is about the size of my little fingernail. Once it's loaded, you just slide the camera open to reveal the lens and viewfinder, then click away. Not much good for distance, but perfect for photographing documents. With it, you can take pictures of the form the renter filled out. Getting the renter's information will be the riskiest part of this job. The quicker you can do it, the better. A photograph will take only a second or two, much faster than writing the information down. And as a bonus, we'll have a sample of his handwriting."

"I warned Grace it might take some sneaking around," Driscoll said.

"*Stealthy* sneaky around, you said," I added.

"Sure you want to do it?" Bobby asked.

"I'm sure. Will the postmaster know what I'm up to?"

Bobby jiggled his head back and forth. "The postmaster can't know. He'd be breaking the law to either give us the name of that renter, or permit us to take it."

"Will I be breaking the law?"

"Well, for a post office employee it'll be more like grounds for dismissal," Bobby said. "But, don't worry. If anything happens, we'll come clean with the postmaster and take full responsibility. Just so you know, Grace, we don't get involved in things illegal, beyond what it sometimes takes to do the job."

I guess they expected me to be worried, but I wasn't. And though I ordinarily don't approve of men who cheat on their wives, Driscoll was right. I liked Bobby Miller immediately. I even went so far as to imagine kissing him. Not that I'd ever do it, mind you, not in a million years. It's this habit I had formulated of imagining myself with every man I meet, related no doubt to Obie rejecting me. Do other people do that? Well,

I find it troubling and, frankly, I'd rather eat my own foot than have anybody find out.

Driscoll caught me staring at his friend. "Anything else on your mind?" he asked with a little half smile. "Have you been to the boarding house yet?"

"No, I came straight here."

"Maudie promised to take good care of you. I stayed at Maudie's for a month when I first moved to Roanoke. Best biscuits I ever ate, better than my grandmother's. And the Sunday dinner rolls ... well, you'll see." He waved a hand at Bobby and at the office in general. "Let me just say that discussing any of this is not for the dining room. Anybody asks what you do, just tell them the truth, you work for the post office. You'll discover that Maudie can be quite a talker," he said with a chuckle, "but she knows you're working for us, she's trustworthy as Fort Knox in that regard and won't say anything about it."

Driscoll glanced at his watch and stood up. "We'll meet here again next Saturday, and every Saturday, Grace. You can report on your week."

Two

There's nothing particularly complicated about me. I'm slightly superstitious and tend to sense things before they happen—traits passed down from my grandmother. Just finished my first year at Stapleton College where I got mixed up in a stolen-money case Piedmont investigated. That's how I met Ray Driscoll. It was exciting stuff for a coed and I took right to it, which is why, when Driscoll offered me a summer job with undercover potential, I jumped at the chance. And I didn't know a thing about the blackmail note yet.

Turns out, Maudie's Boarding House is a rambling two-story brick on Grove Street, just a block off Campbell Avenue, a main thoroughfare.

I pushed on the doorbell and Maudie Patterson herself soon answered. A sturdy woman in a red print dress, dark hair in a bun, lips curved in a smile, eyeglasses on a chain around her neck, and misshapen shoes jutting out on the sides, probably from bunions like my mother's. All business on one hand but nice as can be. "Call me Maudie," she said. "That's what everybody calls me, except the colonel."

She showed me a corner room on the second floor. "Plenty of sun and fresh air from the two sets of double windows," she said, and the curtains waggled in a pleasant breeze as if they were meant to prove it.

Apparently, nobody wanted to pay the steep rent for the big north room. She seemed surprised that I didn't blink or gulp or grimace when she quoted twenty dollars a week. Actually, it was an adventure for me, this living alone for the first time. Twenty a week did not seem so much for a furnished room with meals. Plus, she offered to fix me a bagged lunch each day for an extra three dollars a week.

Money I had inherited from my Aunt Clara permitted this casual view of the rent, and the summer in general. I didn't expect to earn much more than just living expenses, even with the two salaries, but Dad said the experience alone would be like money in the bank.

Maudie rubbed a hand across a corner of the dresser as though checking for dust. "I have room for as many as five lodgers. Right now, there are three others. You'll meet two of them at dinner. Bathroom at each end of the hall. Yours is right next door," she said, pointing. "You'll share it with Clarisse. Let me know if you have any problems with that. Miss Scott and Colonel Fry share the other one."

I nodded and smiled. Two bathrooms for four people. Not bad at all.

"Do you have a telephone?" I asked.

"Yes, of course, the hall table downstairs. We're on a party line with the woman next door—one long ring for her, two short rings for us."

"Will I need a key to get in?"

Maudie shook her head. "There's no need for locks, not here in Roanoke." She turned to go and then paused with a finger across her mouth. "Oh, I should have asked this already. How do you feel about dogs?"

"I love dogs."

"Good. I need to mention Bogart, my terrier. He is accustomed to a free run of the house, so he will come into your room like he owns the place. If that bothers you, just shoo him gently out and shut the door. He'll eventually get the message and leave you alone."

Maudie sent a high school boy to bring the trunk from the car. I shifted my attention to the finer details of the room. A quilt in shades of blue on a bed that appeared overstuffed. Always a good sign, as beds go. A table on each side, one with a radio, the other a lamp. Dresser, chest, closet. A blue plaid chair and footstool that looked like a good place to read.

Bogart showed up in the doorway and stared at me. "Aw, hello, little fellow." I went over to him and held out a hand. He sniffed it, back and front. He was the cutest little black dog—short heavy legs, alert black eyes, ears standing straight up on his head. So different from the dogs in Betula—mostly hounds in some shade of brown, and Betula dogs stay outside.

While I unpacked, Bogart inspected the room. He sniffed the trunk on the floor, the shoes I'd kicked into a corner, my purse hanging on the bedpost, and everything else of mine.

I caught him eyeing the bed. If his legs hadn't been so short, I'm certain he would have leaped up on it. He left the room and returned a minute later with a toy in his mouth. Checking the bed again, he seemed to decide on my reading chair as a better option, jumped onto it without much trouble and settled in to chew his toy and watch me.

Maudie had left an information sheet on the dresser, with check-in and check-out times, and a meal schedule. Three meals a day: 7:30 in the morning, 1:00, and 6:00. Except

Sunday when only two meals were served, at 9:00 in the morning and 4:00.

Clarisse, a pretty blond woman, stopped in and spoke to me. I thought it was nice of her. Bogart, however, dropped his toy and growled. She glared at him. "I can't stand that dog. He has an evil streak." She slipped on a pair of lacy summer gloves, hiding her polished nails in the process. "Well, I'm off to Fletcher's."

"What's Fletcher's?"

"A drugstore. It's the best place you'll find for cosmetics and such." She looked me up and down. "Need anything? Or you could come with me if you want."

"Thanks, but I'd better finish here."

I spent another hour puttering around in my room until Bogart, all at once, abandoned his toy and jumped out of the chair. I knew why. He smelled supper. I followed him downstairs and into the dining room where Maudie was setting the table. She flashed a smile at me and glanced down at the dog. "There you are, Bogey. I wondered where you got off to."

"He was in my room. Can I do something to help?"

"What a nice offer but, no. I'm finishing up here and Gertrude, my housemaid, has things under control in the kitchen. Only four of us this evening. Clarisse will be out again for the night." Maudie cut her eyes at me and anybody could tell she disapproved. The heavy dining table took up much of the room, six chairs around it and space for two more. "Everyone has a designated seat. I'm at the end near the kitchen, and this will be yours, Grace, next to me." Maudie rested a hand on the back of my chair. "Clarisse will be on your other side when she's here. Miss Scott and Colonel Fry sit across the table. She's divorced. He's a pipe-and-slippers bachelor retired from the Army."

"Are they … is there … something between them?"

"Oh, good gracious, no! You'll see how absurd that is. The only thing the colonel and Miss Scott have in common is the same side of the table and the bathroom they share."

The two soon appeared and Maudie introduced me. "Take your seats, everyone, and sweeten your teas. I'll help Gertie with the food."

"No Clarisse again tonight," the colonel said, obviously disappointed at the empty place across from him.

A large platter of porkchops, floured and fried, was set down in the center of the table. Then bowls of parslied potatoes and creamed corn, another of applesauce, served hot.

Almost involuntarily, I said, "Doesn't this look good!"

"Looks very good," said the colonel, rubbing his hands together, impatient to begin. Miss Scott sat placidly with hands in her lap. I decided to copy her.

When Maudie came out of the kitchen, she stood behind her chair and prayed over the table, which was what they'd been waiting for. Then she sat down, pulled up her apron and wiped gravy off her eyeglasses with the hem.

The colonel looked the type to quit on dignity when it came to a meal but he surprised me by taking charge of a perfectly-polite passing of food.

I soon saw what Maudie meant about Miss Scott and the colonel. She, a soft-eyed, quiet-spoken, prim little silver-haired woman who picked at her plate. He, a commanding, thick-necked, heavily-mustached, serious diner with a booming voice, caterpillar eyebrows, hairy ears and enormous appetite.

"Were you in the war, Colonel?" I asked.

"What, you mean this last war? Oh, you flatter me, Miss Dawson."

"Please, call me Grace."

"The Great War was more my game, Grace." He pointed his fork at me. "I see you took that big north room. How old are you? Nineteen, twenty?"

"Nineteen, sir."

"No need to call me sir, young lady, not anymore. Nice and airy, that room, more so than mine. But we'll see how you deal with all the street noise, you and your young ears."

"Street noise?" I asked, glancing at Maudie.

"I had that room once," the colonel went on. "Cars racing by at all hours, and you'll hear the blasted freight train clacking through at midnight."

Maudie said with a tolerant nod, "Grace, the colonel occupies the front room at the other end of the house."

"Yes, and I'm the perfect one for it. My ears are as old as I am. They don't hear street noise so well anymore, and that train isn't near as loud at our end, thank the stars. Can you hear the train in your room, Miss Scott?"

"Just faintly, and I'm accustomed to it now."

Maudie said, "Colonel, if Grace is bothered by the noise, I'll move her to that smaller room in the back."

"All right, Maude, I'll leave it to you, then. What kind of dessert do you have for us tonight?"

"It's peach season, Colonel, so Gertrude has us a fresh peach pie, made it this morning."

"Sounds just fine! Whipped cream?"

"Have you ever known me to serve pie without it?"

"Ha ha ha, Maude, never," the colonel crowed, returning to the creamed corn on his plate.

It would have been unfair to completely hold back compliments, since the food was so darned good. However, I tried not to throw *too* much praise Maudie's way and risk sounding insincere. Part of me wanted to declare it the best I ever ate, and it probably was, it probably was. But to say that would have slighted my mother's many good meals, which wouldn't have been fair, either. I wondered if it was out of the ordinary in some way, something special, like maybe to welcome me.

I woke up in the morning to shreds of cloud and powdery blue sky. The colonel's bothersome street noises had actually appealed to me. The whistling train at midnight, cars traveling by at all hours on their way somewhere. Mixed together, they implied all was well. And this being Sunday, bells tolled in a hundred churches, or so it seemed.

When Bogart whined at the door, I let him in and got a whiff of breakfast.

At nine o'clock, the colonel was already seated at the table sipping coffee. "Good morning. I hope you slept okay in spite of that blasted train. Only two meals on Sundays, Grace, but they're the best of the week, thank the stars."

"Better than last night's?"

"No bread last night, and bread makes all the difference. Doesn't bread make all the difference?" he asked Miss Scott as she took her chair.

"Yes, colonel," she said, smiling at me instead of him. "Otherwise, there's nothing for you to put your butter on."

Maudie came through the swinging kitchen door with a hot platter in each hand, set them on the table and winked at me. Then she went through again and came back balancing bowls. It felt wrong to just sit there and not offer help—my training at home.

We had fruit in front of us, eggs and bacon and sausage, a platter of the biscuits Driscoll liked so much. To go with those biscuits, a bowl of gravy (a favorite of mine, sorry to say) and two kinds of preserves.

15

We started without Clarisse, the others seeming to know she wouldn't show up. I didn't expect her either, after hearing her come in late at night.

"Is Gertrude here this morning?" I asked.

"No, she's off on Sundays, and Monday mornings, too, until noon."

All the more reason for me to offer assistance after breakfast. But it did me no good.

I put on a hat and gloves and went to church with Maudie and Miss Scott. When we got home, Maudie was soon working on four o'clock dinner. I popped my head in the kitchen, asked if I could help and wondered if lodgers were supposed to stay out of there. She glanced up from peeling potatoes and shook her head. Something already smelled good.

Sunday dinner was a one-pot wonder—a hardy beef roast and vegetables. Good choice for Maudie, working alone. The main attraction turned out to be yeast rolls just out of the oven, reserved only for Sundays, mounded in a silver bowl with a linen-napkin cover to keep them hot. I was shocked to see the colonel cut off a plug of butter as big as my fist and divide it evenly amongst four rolls. Everybody else seemed unaffected, evidently accustomed to such behavior.

Clarisse joined us this time, dressed to go out again, it looked like. She added tang to the table, flirted outrageously with the aging colonel who got younger from her attention and busty-blond good looks. He seemed to swallow whole whatever she said. With her there, we carried on a lively conversation, the five of us, discussing everything from Dragnet to the atomic bomb.

Over dessert—a delicious peach, gingersnaps and custard concoction—I stole glances at Clarisse to try and guess her age. Late twenties, I figured.

Afterward, I lagged behind and carried dishes without permission. "Oh, you don't need to do that, dear," Maudie said. But I kept it up.

After dinner, to acquaint myself with the roads, I climbed in the car and took a practice ride to the post office. After that I played with the camera up in my room, snapped a picture of the oil painting on the wall and another of my shoes.

Three

Driscoll had said to show up on the job at nine. Maudie handed me a bagged lunch Monday morning, fixed the collar of my white blouse and shooed me out the door in time to arrive a few minutes early, like any self-respecting new employee. I drove over there with chewing gum in my mouth, which helped settle nerves, I had learned.

The Salem Post Office sits at the corner of Main Street and Market in the middle of downtown. If you count the parking lot, it takes up nearly a whole city block, all the way back to Clay.

A sidewalk and steps took me to the front entrance, two cast iron lampposts and a blue mailbox rising out of the cement, and the United States flag on a pole. The post office hours are nine to five so I stood out there, chewed my gum and waited for the place to open. Others soon gathered. Couldn't tell whether they were customers, or more new employees, until a man unlocked the doors and they brushed right by with a purpose instead of acting lost like me.

With the camera deep in my pocket I paused in the vestibule to look at Wanted posters on the bulletin board and a portrait of President Eisenhower on the wall. I passed through to the lobby where all the business gets done, and on my first look at this grand old post office, I just stood there and stared. Highest ceiling I ever saw, skylight in the center to let the sun pour in as much as it would. And the floors! Imagine my surprise finding black, white and pink marble underfoot. Immense and dignified, this post office seemed more fit for something else, like a museum maybe, to exhibit statues and rare finds. Quite a departure from the tiny one at home, doing the same job for probably just as long a time in the Betula Drugstore.

As my eyes traveled the lobby I saw clear signs of the services you'd expect—doors marked POSTMASTER and MONEY ORDERS and SPECIAL DELIVERY, counter window with a shiny brass grille, mail slots for Local and Out of Town, two chest-high writing tables each with a glass top and built-in inkwell, one of those little stamp machines you put money in, and scores of numbered lockboxes lined up on the widest wall. When my eyes got there they stayed. I took a step or two in that direction and soon spotted the one thing most central to this job—lockbox 45—between the right side and the middle, and halfway down. They all had glass doors like the ones at the college, and I could see from mid-lobby that the box in question had nothing in it but air.

I smiled out loud, pleased with myself for such quick progress. I know, I know. Finding the lockbox wasn't much of a feat. But the smile wasn't wasted, as it turned out, put to good service when the foreman, Mr. Acres, introduced himself and assumed it was for him. He walked me around the lobby, pointing out things I had already noticed. Then he took me to meet the postmaster sitting behind a piled-up desk with a telephone at his ear. His nameplate said, Waldo T. Whitney.

As we stood there filling up the doorway, he gave us a smile and a nod, then turned away in a kind of dismissal.

Mr. Acres opened a door marked Employees Only and we walked through. "This is the workroom where all your time will be spent. Every service offered in the lobby is supported back here." He introduced me to Roberta, wedding band on her finger, long hair in tight curls. "She's a sorting clerk like you. She'll teach you the job."

The first thing Roberta did was lead me up a set of spiral stairs to the attic. The postal employees have an area up there, with lockers and a bathroom, and tables where you can sit and eat. I put my purse and lunch bag in the locker assigned to me, and we went back down to the workroom.

After a few minutes of watching, I saw what Mr. Acres meant by supporting lobby services. The mail slots spilled out into bins back there, the counter clerk stood at the window back there, and rolling metal doors opened out to the loading docks back there.

The workroom was L-shaped. The long leg was all about sorting the mail—tabletops crowded with baskets, floor cluttered with hampers on wheels. Most important to me, though, was the short leg of the workroom, which wrapped right around behind that lockbox wall so mail could be inserted from back there.

Roberta and I handled only outgoing mail the first day. It came in a continuous stream from the lobby, and twice-a-day pickup from the blue mailboxes around town, including the one in front of the post office.

The idea was to sort the mail into three categories (local, out of town, out of state). Of course, it wasn't as simple as that, but no reason to bore you with all the details here. Let me just say that we separated local into two groups—delivery and lockbox. Yeah, lockbox. This part obviously excited me.

My excitement disappeared, however, when Roberta said it was not Outgoing's job to pigeonhole (that's what they call it) the lockbox mail. It was Incoming's job. All we had to do was throw it into the Pigeon Local bin. I was able to quickly check for box 45 on the letters I handled, but what about Roberta? What about everybody else?

As for the other categories, we wrapped bundles of them in twine, marked each with the correct sticker, then tossed the bundle into the correct hamper. Full hampers we just shoved toward the loading dock, except for local delivery, which stayed right there. Easy. The job could be done without much thought, which left me to observe and ponder.

Every few minutes I wanted to reach in my pocket for the camera. The feeling was strong, like the urge to pick at a hangnail, and seemed just as bad an idea.

I found a key from the Richmond Hotel in a mailbox pickup and pointed it out as odd. But Roberta said it happens all the time. Somebody stays in a hotel, takes the key by mistake and drops it into a mailbox. We just treat it like any other outgoing mail and send it back.

According to Roberta, surprising things are often discovered in mailboxes. Her finds so far had been a dead chipmunk and a pack of caramel creams. The best in anyone's memory was a genuine ruby ring in a velvet box, discovered a week before Christmas one year. Worth five hundred dollars, or so the story goes.

A little after five I picked up my purse from the attic locker, gazed one more time at the overflowing Pigeon Local bin waiting for the Incoming clerks, and hoped that better luck and Mr. Acres would let me be an Incoming clerk the next day.

But Tuesday was a copy of the first for Roberta and me. And Wednesday, too, had a frustrating similarity. I ended that day, however, with new understanding. Mr. Acres had assigned me to Outgoing mail and that's where I'd stay. I was a dunce not to see it sooner. Incoming clerks keep a different schedule (seven until three) to deal with the trucks arriving early in the morning and again around noon. To have any chance at all, I somehow had to switch.

It was remarkably easy, the way it turned out.

On Thursday morning, Roberta told me most workers don't like the early schedule, so I simply asked Mr. Acres if I could maybe trade with somebody.

At first, the idea seemed doomed. He looked up from his clipboard and shook his head. "You're a poor fit for Incoming. That's why we put you here. Incoming requires knowing the routes, the mailman routes. A good Incoming clerk must know them all. You are temporary, Miss Dawson, and new to Salem. By the time you get the hang of it, you'll be gone. Where's the sense in that?"

At lunchtime I made my way to a nearby park and sat on a bench to eat and think. Out of Maudie's bag came a thick ham sandwich, an oatmeal cookie and a cut-up peach. I ate the sandwich facing the fact that this assignment was going to be harder than ever expected. I shared the peach with a begging squirrel and put away the cookie for later.

On the short walk back to the post office, I summed up my bleak situation: No mail for the lockbox yet, at least none I had seen. We needed the name of that lockbox renter and I'd made no headway there, either. Driscoll had said to be sneaky and just look in the file. Okay, but first I needed to know where they kept it and I couldn't just ask. So, into my fourth day already and no progress at all.

Then, out of the blue, Mr. Acres changed his mind. Don't know why, exactly, but it changed everything for me. I could switch to Incoming and be the primary pigeon-holer, he said. No complicated training needed there. I was to pigeonhole all day, and when I ran out of stuff to pigeon, I could help with Outgoing. He put me on it immediately.

The primary pigeonholer! What could be better? It certainly improved my lot. I pigeonholed letters from the noontime truck, plus the bin from Pigeon Local that kept filling up. At the end of the day, though, there was still no mail for, well, you know the one.

Bogart greeted me at the door after work and followed me up the stairs. I saw how it was for him. Maudie was always in the kitchen at that time and he wasn't allowed in there when food was getting fixed. Miss Scott and the colonel were a couple of door closers and Bogart did not like Clarisse.

He immediately sniffed out that leftover cookie in my purse and seemed to pout when I wouldn't give it to him. I doubt Maudie would have approved if I had given it to him (bad for his teeth and all) but frankly, I didn't like him well enough yet to share such a cookie—fat moist raisins in it and chopped-up pecans.

I closed the door to change my clothes and tell Bogart about my day. Well, whyever not? I wasn't allowed to discuss it with anyone else and he was a good listener, tilting his head this way and that as he tried to understand.

While I talked, the idea hit me to rent a lockbox myself! Renting one would give me a chance to study the setup, find out where they kept that file. Plus, checking my own lockbox would give me an added excuse to be over that way, especially if they assigned me one nearby. I thanked the good listener for his help and made a mental note to study the lockbox wall layout.

On Friday morning I did just that and decided on number 44 or 55. No mail had come in for either of those in my one afternoon of pigeonholing. I know it didn't mean much but it was all I had, and time melted away.

Lockbox assignment was part of the counter clerk's job. I knew that much. Kenny, a man with a toothy grin, filled that spot most of the time, part of the friendly workroom chatter.

My plan was to get the lockbox first thing during lunch break and worry about eating afterward. But Kenny had gone to lunch himself by then, replaced by Grace Contee. I had seen her around. In fact, on my first day, I watched her slide a letter into her pocket and wondered why she did it.

I sidled over to her, timing it with a brief lull in her line. "We haven't met yet but we share the same first name," I said with a smile.

"I know who you are," she said grumpily, narrowing her eyes. Made me wonder if I'd done something wrong.

"I would like to rent a lockbox, please."

"If you want counter service, get in the counter line." She jabbed a finger toward the lobby.

"But, there is no line at the moment," I sweetly stated the obvious.

"You need to be out there, regardless."

Now, that was a problem. I had to be next to her in order to watch. "Oh, okay, thanks," I said, walking in confusion. More than once, I had seen Kenny help an employee who was standing right there. All afternoon I kept an eye out for him. When three o'clock came and went, it was clear he had gone for the day.

So, to sum things up, I ended my entire first week with no more than when I started. No name for the renter, no mail in the lockbox, not a thing to report at the Saturday meeting. Oh, hell.

Driscoll, however, believed that not finding any mail might be telling us something. It could mean Bobby's letter was the only one sent, that it might be actual blackmail. It was enough to scare our remorseful philanderer right out of his shoes.

Four

Saturday afternoon I was involved in an accident. Or rather, just my car. A man in a bakery truck swerved to keep from hitting a boy on a bike and in doing so, slammed into my car and two others parked in front of Leggett's Department Store. I was among the many pouring out the doors to check the commotion. And there it was—my beautiful Chevy that Dad bought me in eleventh grade—shoved up on the sidewalk in a steaming, twisted pile.

Taking everything into account, though, things weren't so bad. The boy ran straight home to mother, and the truck driver went back to delivering doughnuts the next day. But it didn't do those cars any good at all.

Driscoll volunteered to be my transportation until I could get another vehicle. On Monday morning I learned a few things about him on the way to work. His mother died two years ago, father lives in Richmond, sister is married with kids and lives in Tennessee. His first car was an old jalopy he bought right after the war, paid thirty-five dollars for it and it was worth that much back then just for the tires. He enjoys the funny papers on Sundays, particularly *Moon Mullins*, and claims not to have a favorite color.

We got to the post office early so I could rent that lockbox, which turned out to be easy as pie. Before the counter window opened for the day, Kenny helped me while I stood in the workroom beside him.

"Is number forty-four available, or maybe fifty-five?" I asked. He studied me over the top of his glasses. "Easy to remember," I quickly added.

"Six-month lease or a year?"

"Six-month."

"That'll be four dollars."

While I reached in my purse for the money, he opened the drawer to his left, thumbed through cards in a wooden box, removed one and handed it to me. "You're in luck. Forty-four is available. Put your name, home address and telephone number. Then, sign it and you'll be in business."

I did what he said using Maudie's as home. When I handed it back, he filed the card in the box where it came from, reached into an open safe under the counter, grabbed a key from a board and placed it in my hand.

"Being an employee, I don't really need this key, do I?"

"Yeah, you do. You must remove your mail from the front like everyone else. Technically, you're a customer when it comes to this lockbox, and mail must be in there before you can take it out."

I gave him a questioning look and got ready to speak, but he put up a hand. "Yes, I know, even if you're the one who pigeonholes it. Might sound silly but those are the rules. It helps keep things straight and above any questions."

That little encounter gave me a glow for the rest of the morning and all afternoon. When I told Driscoll, he called it good work. All I needed next, he said, was opportunity to break in the file.

That evening, to prepare myself, I played with the Minox again, captured the *Carpe Diem* plaque on the door without knowing what it meant, and then the fancy doily on the dresser.

The following days found me searching for opportunity and coming upon none. Seemed like Kenny was always there—arrived ahead, left after, and never stepped away until grumpy Grace took over. Maybe it was nerves or my inexperience, but no time felt right.

Here's what Driscoll had to say about it Thursday on the way home: "That's okay. It's smart to wait. You'll get your chance and when you do, just be ready, be alert. Then plow straight ahead without fear or thought. And, for heaven's sake, no guilty glancing around. That's a killer in this game." His words made me feel better and lasted the whole evening.

But Friday during an honest appraisal, my cheeriness sank. The entire second week was looking like a bust, with still no letters for the lockbox, no chance yet to look in the file. And a chance wasn't likely to present itself, either, on a busy Friday afternoon.

Then, around two o'clock, I actually found a letter! Straight out of the Pigeon Local bin. I was lucky to be alone behind the wall, the way I reacted with glee. Not to mention how I studied the envelope, held it up to the light, then slipped the Minox out of my pocket and took a quick picture. It was addressed the way the letter said, with no return address, and looked like it contained a fold of money. I had often dreamed as a kid of following a shiny trail of coins leading to a thousand quarters piled high behind a bush. It felt just like that.

In a little pocket notebook, I recorded the date and the fact it came from local, mailed in town. Then I put a tiny pencil-dot on the back of the envelope down in a corner. Don't exactly know why. I wanted to take the actual letter with me to show Driscoll, but I just did my job and pigeonholed it.

When Driscoll picked me up around four he could see I was all a-bubble. When I told him he just smiled and offered his usual, "Good work." That was okay. I was accustomed by then to his subdued reactions. Truth was, you couldn't tell a thing about what Driscoll really felt— not by what he said, anyway. You needed to gauge it from the sparkle in his eyes, and he showed plenty there.

The question was whether to go tell Bobby immediately or wait until the morning meeting. We decided on the sooner, knowing the news would be a gift to him of a good night's sleep.

When we got to the Piedmont office, Bobby was sitting at the table with two other people, strangers to me. We must have been as easy to read as a billboard, the way he excused himself, hopped right up and joined us in the hall.

Bobby laughed out loud when I told him and slapped his knee. Then he danced me around, kissed my hand and came close to shedding tears. In a matter of seconds, he looked like a new man. Only one letter, but it was what the letter implied—that the whole ugly business was a bluff.

I mentioned the picture I took of the envelope, but nobody could name a benefit of having the victim's handwriting, not even me.

"Now, what *would* be beneficial," Driscoll said, "is if you could see the guy open the lockbox. And if you could get a picture of him, it would really be wonderful. Any chance of that?"

I hated to disappoint him but, hardly any chance at all. In the workroom, I rarely get to witness anything customers do. And worse, the lobby never closes. A person could walk in anytime to put mail in the slot, buy stamps from the machine, or check a lockbox. I explained all this, feeling a bit dejected.

Driscoll realized he had asked too much. "Sorry, Grace. I'm such an ungrateful clod. You gave us the moon on a platter and I wanted the stars."

Five

The next day, Saturday, they decided our usual meeting wasn't necessary so Driscoll took me car shopping instead. He offered to spend the whole day running from dealer to dealer with me. I could afford most any make — Pontiac, Buick, or even Cadillac, but Chevrolet was the only one I cared about.

When it comes to automobiles, I follow my dad. He believes in sensibly-priced cars, and a new one if it's in the budget, to avoid buying somebody else's trouble. He prefers Chevrolets. Therefore, so do I, and they are fine-looking cars on the road.

At the Chevy dealer we first strolled around outside, but it was too blasted hot to stay out there long. We read a few stickers, opened a few doors as heat radiated from hoods, sun reflected off windshields and chrome, all of it hot to the touch.

By the time we entered the showroom, I had already made up my mind. I wanted a mid-range model with a factory-installed radio and electric clock.

A salesman soon approached us wearing a grin. While he talked cars with Driscoll, I attempted to size him up. The nametag on his gray suit said, Norm Nelson. Good name for a salesman. Brown hair combed straight back, puckered pink scar on one cheek, smudge of toothpaste on the other, and an Adam's apple that stuck way out. I couldn't read his eyes.

Driscoll finally nodded in my direction. "I'm not the one buying it. She is."

"Oh, I'm sorry," Norm said, turning to me.

By this time, my eyes were on a red Bel Air going around in circles on a platform, shiny as a Christmas tree. The salesman noticed, probably smelling the big sale of the day. To tell the truth, I'd never seen anything so tempting. For a moment I did want that car, but it was more about the rotating platform it stood on.

Driscoll wandered over for a closer look. Giving me space to make my own deal, I figured.

Norm scratched the side of his head and smoothed back his hair as I told him what all I wanted in a car. "We have two of those in stock, a dark blue one and ... I believe the other is yellow. Of course, you can order one in any color you choose and we'll have it here in two months." He said this proudly, following with a smile.

"I need a car now."

He scratched his head again and smoothed back his hair. "But, we won't be able to arrange financing that fast," he said, as though it ought to be obvious.

"I don't need financing. Can't I just write a check?"

"Well, yeah."

I settled on a 210 model for $1700, a pale yellow sedan with shiny black trim, push-button factory radio, arm rests, and electric clock. Not as luxurious on the inside as the more expensive Bel Air. Not as much chrome, either, but the amount it had was enough for me—bumpers, front grille and hood ornament.

Norm Nelson turned out to be a fine salesman once he got the hang of dealing with me. Although, I wondered about all that head scratching and hair smoothing. Was it a scalp condition? A nervous tic?

My 210 was a peach of a car, even Driscoll said so. I drove it off the lot with a grin as broad as Norm's, my new tires humming on the road. But it meant not riding with the ungrateful clod anymore, and that part was sad.

Back at the boarding house I found a letter from Mother and sat down with it on a parlor couch. It was a short letter, not one of her rambling ones but more to the point. She wanted me home for Independence Day weekend. Obie might be there, too, apparently, which caused my heart to gain speed. Not only that, Mother said he had asked about me. Now, those words had power. I could feel it already, hope bubbling up that Obie had changed his mind.

The wind billowed the curtains and felt good on my skin. Shutting my eyes, I chewed my gum and tried not to dwell on home. I could hear backyard noises—towels snapping on the clothesline, Bogart woofing so much at something (probably a squirrel) that Gertrude had to call him in.

Maudie came out of her private apartment and sat next to me. I had not yet been invited in there but knew it stretched beyond the parlor through paneled double doors. She patted me on the arm. "Would you like some iced tea?" She didn't wait for an answer, just went to the kitchen and came back carrying two frosty glasses on a tray. I nearly drank mine straight down, thirsty as I was. She, by comparison, took a dainty sip and set hers aside.

"Your father called," she said. "He's returning home from Richmond tomorrow and wants to come for a visit. I insisted he stay for dinner and spend the night. He can have the extra bedroom."

I reached over and pushed a loose hairpin back into her bun. "Are you sure you don't mind?"

"Of course, I don't mind. I invited him, didn't I? Stopping here is important enough that he's going out of his way to do it. Hmm, Shepherd's Pie is on the menu for tomorrow and fried chicken tonight. I'm going to switch them."

"Oh Maudie, fried chicken is my daddy's favorite. Mine, too, for that matter."

"You don't need to tell me that, being from the south."

"Yeah, everybody in Betula has fried chicken on Sunday. Only, they go out in the back and kill one instead of buying it in a store."

"Don't need to tell me that, either. I probably chopped off the heads of a hundred chickens in my time."

"But, you're choosing such a messy dinner on a night without Gertrude. I remember the kitchen at home after a meal such as that—flour on the floor, greasy frying pan, and a pot with dried potato stuck to it."

"I know, but I'm doing it for your dad."

I told her about the letter.

"Do you want to go home for the holiday?" she asked.

"I can't go home. I honestly cannot afford to miss a single day at the post office right now. Isn't next Saturday July fourth?"

"Well then, good, you'll stay here with us. The Chamber of Commerce parade goes right down Campbell Avenue and I've been known to make homemade ice cream. How does that sound?"

"Sounds just fine. Betula doesn't have enough people to make a decent parade. If they ever tried, there'd be nobody left to watch. But they always have a picnic on the high school lawn, and folks back home are experts when it comes to ice cream."

"Would you want to go home if you could?"

"Well, I guess I'm afraid."

"Afraid? What could you be afraid of?"

"Obie broke up with me last spring and I'm still trying to get over it. What if he *is* there? What if he wants me back? Seeing him will stir up that hurt all over again, I know it."

"It's none of my business but, gosh-a-mighty, a pretty girl like you? All you need is a sweetheart or two knocking at the door. Not all men are like this Obie. Some are solid and trustworthy. My husband, George, was one of them. There will be somebody like that for you." She put her hand on top of mine and squeezed. "I think you ought to hold out."

Maudie soon left to help Gertrude in the kitchen. I headed upstairs. Bogart trailed after me and arranged himself in my reading chair. He watched me change clothes and fought a losing battle with sleep until I went downstairs again. In the dining room he curled up in a corner beside a potted plant while I helped Maudie set the table.

"I wonder what it's like to be blond," I said, thinking out loud. "Maybe Obie would have stayed around if I were a blond like Clarisse."

"You mean, a bleached blond."

"Clarisse has bleached hair?"

Maudie held up her hands. "I don't make a practice of talking about my lodgers, but of course it's bleached! Do you want bleached hair?"

"No."

"Well, then …"

"Will she be here for dinner?"

"Nah, she's rarely home for Saturday dinner, her big night to prowl. It's none of my business, but you've seen what a flirt she is."

If Maudie was referring to Clarisse's dealings with the colonel, I thought it was sweet. "Is she looking for a husband?"

"Looking for a husband? Lord, what a question! Nothing to do with me, but of course, she is!"

"How old is she, about twenty-five?"

"Gawd, she's older than that! I don't normally tell tales about my lodgers, though in this case I happen to know she's only ten years younger than me, which puts her at thirty-two. But, I don't like to talk." She disappeared into the kitchen and came back a few seconds later with salt-and-pepper shakers. "Except, Clarisse dresses too young and flashy for somebody her age, if you ask me. Especially at work."

"Where does she work?"

"Courthouse, in the Records office. Hoping to catch herself a lawyer in there, been trying for years. With that kind of job, she ought to dress more dignified. But I don't say a word."

I didn't say a word, either. Every time I saw Clarisse leave for work in the morning, she looked pretty good. A bit flashy, maybe, but pretty-danged good. Actually, in my opinion, Clarisse tends most carefully to her appearance. She's sloppy about everything else, however. Her untidy room, for instance. Walking down the hall, I see it. Unmade bed, trash cans full and running over, dresses flung across furniture instead of hanging up. In the parlor, she drops chewing-gum wrappers in little wads on the floor and leaves half-empty pop bottles with no more fizz to make rings on the side tables. Maudie hasn't said a word about any of that, at least not to me, but maybe it's because Gertrude is the one who gets stuck cleaning it up.

Six

Later, in the cool of Saturday evening, Maudie put a leash on Bogart and we went for a stroll.

"The Independence Day parade comes right down Campbell Avenue, just a block that way," she said, pointing behind us. "The only thing better would be if it turned and came by my front porch. Did I tell you the colonel will be in it?"

"Why, no!"

"He rides in it every year, part of the military brigade. It's his favorite thing in the whole world, so we make a fuss over him."

Bogart tugged on his leash at the sidewalk next door. "Nothing doing, boy. You know you're not allowed." Maudie dragged the dog away. "He has a girlfriend in there. We discovered them together in the back yard last winter when Ethel left her gate open. Five of the cutest puppies you ever saw came from that little visit. We share the party line with Ethel, by the way."

"Maudie, I've been wondering. How did you get into the boarding house business?"

"Well, it was everything to do with losing George. When I got the telegram that he had been killed, I cried for a week. Looking back, it was as much about facing the future without a husband as losing him. My family was poor, growing up. Daddy died and Mother did her best, but we never had anything much. I recall Christmases when her best meant decorating an empty coffee can with holly sprigs and a page ripped out of an old magazine. I was afraid I'd sink that low again without a man. Then, Ethel said I ought to use this big house to my advantage and take in boarders. So that's what I did. Been doing just fine ever since."

"You're a natural for it, Maudie, seems to me."

"Why, thank you, Grace," she said, patting my arm. "The country is full of war widows. I'm not one to talk out of turn, but we've got several on this street. Ethel's a widow living alone, except for her dog. She has gracefully accepted her fate. Others are still looking, poor things. In the house next to Ethel we've got a single man of about thirty. Parents both dead. He came back from the war with a permanent limp. Nice man, though, a good catch for somebody. Clarisse tried her luck but he wasn't interested. Too brassy for him, I imagine. Nice men just don't like that sort of thing." Maudie shook her head in disapproval. "Clarisse tried her luck with Driscoll, too, early on. Did you know that? He was attracted at first, like any man would be to flirty ways and flashy clothes. But that kind of attraction doesn't last. I knew she wasn't right for him and I could have told him so, except he didn't ask and I don't like to pry."

"How old is Driscoll?"

"Twenty-eight."

Definitely too old for me, then, I thought sadly. "Isn't it funny. We both call him Driscoll instead of Ray or Mr. Driscoll."

"Well, that's how he introduces himself to people. I've heard him. 'My name's Driscoll,' he says."

"I believe you're right. That's what he said to me when we first met. Has he had many girlfriends?"

"A few." Maudie pointed across the street to a brick house that looked a lot like hers. "The woman over there? Now, she was a widow who actually found a husband. But then, she had money, and a woman with money is always a target for a fortune hunter."

"Are you saying her husband was a fortune hunter?"

"I'm not saying that exactly, and it's none of my affair. Except, she would have been better off without him, if you ask me. What did she need a man for? Certainly not for support, and this one has chicken feathers for brains and falls down a lot when he drinks."

Nobody around here knows about the inheritance I share with my little cousin, Henry, not even Driscoll. Dad convinced me to keep it to myself. Over fifty thousand dollars in cash and stocks, plus a house in Betula and an office building in Abingdon. Not enough to attract one of those fortune hunters, maybe, but I don't want to worry about any man being interested in me because of it. I could never accuse Obie of that. He knows all about it and still doesn't want me.

That night, he visited me in a fuzzy dream. At least, I felt it was him and wondered what it meant. Maybe we appeal to him again, me and Betula. Maybe someday he'll confess what happened. I bet he got burned.

I expected Maudie to at least scratch the dinner rolls off the Sunday menu since they cause such a mess themselves, but by the time I came down ready for church, she had already set the dough to rise in a covered bowl.

I offered to take her in my new car, just the two of us because Miss Scott was off visiting her brother. It was going to be another hot day. We had to roll down all the windows to let the air blow through.

After the service, we made for home so Maudie could start dinner.

"Let me show you a way to avoid all this traffic," she said, as I turned onto Campbell Avenue. "Turn right just ahead. See the alley? You can pick up Turner Street on the other side and cut off that busy corner."

The alley took us behind Piggly Wiggly. This being Sunday, it was deserted back there.

Maudie pointed to a man in a far corner. "What's that man doing? Usually there's nobody back here but birds. Oh, I see, he's putting on a license plate."

There was something familiar about him. I slowed down for a better look and he chose that moment to scratch his head and smooth back his hair.

"Oh, I know him. He's the Chevrolet salesman who sold me this car yesterday." I got ready to wave from a distance but he never looked up. "That's odd, don't you think? Why's he doing it back here?"

"Well, he has to do it some place. Car salesmen probably switch license plates all the time."

"Why not at the dealer? Plenty of room there, and that's a Chevy he's working on."

"It isn't a new car, though. Looks just like mine except for the color."

"They sell used cars, too."

Maudie glanced over her shoulder and out the window. "I like the look of that one. Never thought much of black cars, with so many of them on the road. Next time, though, I might change my mind. You know, Grace, it could be his own car."

"Yeah, but if that's the case, why is he putting them on now? It isn't the right time for license plates. Virginia won't be issuing new ones for months yet."

"Oh, I don't know. He must have some reason."

"Yeah, but–"

"I can see why Driscoll hired you, that inquisitive nature of yours."

I dropped the subject with Maudie. It wasn't getting me anywhere. But, why *would* the salesman choose the back side of Piggly Wiggly to put a license plate on a car. And why would he be doing it at all, when it wasn't renewal time. It just didn't add up. A strong feeling hit me that I was supposed to take that detour, something back there I was supposed to see. This line of thinking gave me mild willy symptoms—goosebumps and a tingling between my eyes, which grew worse a few minutes later up in my room at the sight of the little camera and the sneaky part of my assignment yet to come.

I would have chewed on that all afternoon if not for my father's visit. There were five of us planned for dinner, with my father and without Miss Scott. Maudie said to use the best china and to put Dad at the vacant place at the end, between Clarisse and the colonel.

I took charge of the potatoes—peeling, cooking, mashing. Couldn't very well let Maudie handle it all, especially since she was doing it for my dad.

I was in and out of the kitchen while she fried her chicken in the two biggest frying pans I ever saw, and then used one of them for gravy. Oh, what a mess we made! We left it all to deal with later as we carried the platters into the dining room. Just before going through, Maudie wiped gravy off her glasses with her apron hem. Her cheeks were flushed from kitchen heat as she offered up the prayer. I thought she looked adorable.

We had a merry time, so I guess it was worth the effort. I must say, though, Clarisse's forward behavior annoyed me when pointed at my dad. All during dinner, she'd lean over and put a hand on his arm to ask a thoughtful question, mostly about the law. Then, she'd listen to his answer with frequent nods and wide-eyed interest. She must have asked a dozen questions and I bet she already knew the answers, having that courthouse job. But she appears to be a master at dealing with men so I could learn a few things from her. Even my father seemed charmed.

After a simple orange sherbet dessert, the colonel suggested a brandy and pulled Dad into the parlor. The kitchen had to be dealt with and I felt compelled to help, even with Maudie's protests. When the last pan had been put in a cupboard, the last counter wiped clean, I escaped the kitchen and thought of Gertrude, wondering what it must be like to deal every day with dishpan hands and chores that don't stay done.

I stole Dad away from the colonel and we walked outside. I told him about the accident, showed him my new car. We relaxed in rocking chairs on one end of the front porch. There was so much to tell him that nobody else could hear—about the blackmail note and the real purpose of the job. I did not mention sneaking into the file, even as it weighed on my mind. Better to tell him later, after the job was done, because he wouldn't have liked the sound of it.

I talked on and on without a pause. It never occurred to me that he had something to say until he patted my hand and gave me a few quick nods. That's what he's always done to make me stop and listen.

"I saw Obie in Richmond," he said, "ran into him in a cafe."

"Oh. Did you talk to him? How is he?"

"Seems fine. He was with a girl."

"Oh."

"He asked me to join them, just being polite. I declined. It would have been an awkward meal."

"But, Mother wrote and said he asked about me …"

"Perhaps he did, but the two of them seemed more than just friends, Gracie, too busy with each other to even notice me at first."

I took a sharp breath and we both sat still and quiet. Finally, he squeezed my arm and ran a hand up and down it. "Anyway, I thought you ought to know."

"What kind of person is she? What does she look like?" I hated to ask.

He thought for a moment. "Well, in both manner and appearance, I'd say a lot like Clarisse a few years back."

My heart sank to the bottom and stayed down there. With a case of the blues and dreading tomorrow, I lay in bed listening to street noises and pondered bleaching my hair. I told myself there'd soon be another man for me, maybe even in one of those cars passing by. I was still awake at two in the morning when the wind, calm one minute and gusting the next, blew the lid off a garbage can and hurled it down the street.

Seven

After a restless night, I got up early to see Dad on his way. He left five dollars on the dresser in his room, always one to do the right thing. It was a dull Monday morning, weather-wise—cloudy and dark to fit my mood.

I drove on ahead to work, figuring the best hope to sneak in the file would be before anybody else got there. It was only six-thirty when I went in through the side entrance. The janitor was busy cleaning the lobby floor.

The workroom had an empty silence at first until I heard somebody moving around behind the lockbox wall. Grumpy Grace was back there for some reason. Hard to say which one of us was more surprised. And, I'll tell you something else: She was definitely up to something. You could see it in her eyes. Even made me wonder if she might be the blackmail renter.

Seeing me, she grabbed her purse in a huff, made for the attic stairs and left me standing alone. But, this was no time to sneak into the file, not with her upstairs and fixing to come down. Instead, I simply checked the lockbox to find Friday's letter still there, then went to work pigeonholing. I was well into the job when the early truck rolled in at seven.

By noon, the sky threatened rain. I carried my lunch over to the park bench anyway and ate with the squirrels. On the walk back I got a mean case of the willys, warning me of, well, I didn't know what. I reached in my purse for a fresh stick of doublemint and a minute or so later, on the sidewalk, I passed a man holding an envelope up like he was trying to see into it. The envelope had a lumpy familiarity.

I know, I know. What was the chance of him being the very man with the very letter. I turned and stared at him anyhow, made mental notes as he continued down the sidewalk. Then, I followed him. Yeah, I followed him. It was starting to rain, but I stuck with the guy to the parking lot and watched him climb into a battered blue Plymouth. The easy rain swelled to a storm on the way back. I covered my head with the empty lunch bag and ran.

I knew it was him, just knew it, especially after finding an empty lockbox. I escaped to the attic bathroom and jotted down notes about the man: Medium height and build, brown hair, plaid shirt, walks with a limp, old blue Plymouth.

The storm continued. It blew so much rain in through the loading dock that the mail got wet and they were forced to pull down the doors. It didn't take long for the workroom to get hot and stuffy as we bustled around in there.

Then, just before three o'clock, we heard that somebody robbed the Salem Union Bank. A man with a gun, the radio said. The license-plate scene I had witnessed on Sunday popped into my head, but not for long.

A half-hour later, as if that weren't enough, I found another letter. Not so thrilling as the first one, or as important, but I treated it the same—marked it with a pencil dot and recorded it in the notebook.

After work, with so much to report, I telephoned Driscoll on a drugstore pay phone. The second letter pleased him and he passed the news to Bobby who was sitting right there. About the man I saw, though, neither believed he was the blackmailer.

Then, Driscoll asked, "Anything else? Any progress on that renter form?"

"Not yet. Still waiting for a chance," I said with a thud.

I'm sure he didn't like the sound of it because, well, neither did I. It sounded so lame.

At the dinner table that evening, first thing after passing the platters, Miss Scott looked my way and said, "Grace, I have a nephew I want you to meet. His name is Wesley, my brother's son. Nice-looking young man about your age. He wants to meet a girl and I thought of you."

Maudie threw a glance in my direction.

"And who wouldn't want to meet such a dark-haired beauty," the colonel added, his heavy head cocked to one side.

"Yes, and Wesley would be a fine catch, too," Miss Scott added. "He's done so well for himself. Just moved here from Wytheville to take up a position at Leggett's Department Store." An important position, she called it, without really saying what it was.

Blind dates were foreign to me but I accepted this one for reasons still blurry. Miss Scott got on the telephone after dessert and had the whole thing arranged in minutes. Her nephew and I were going to dinner Friday, he'd pick me up at seven. At least we had one thing in common. We were both new in town.

But don't let me pretend disinterest. Truth is, I had high hopes, thought about it all evening and tried to decide on what to wear. Maybe Maudie was right. All I needed was another man to push Obie out of my head, and Wesley might be the one.

On Tuesday I got to work even earlier hoping to get the dreaded job done. I couldn't stand the thought of Driscoll disappointed in me. But grumpy Grace had shown up before me again, doing something behind the lockbox wall. We seemed to be in a contest for who could be first in the morning, both of us in need of secrecy. My need was sneaky and scheming but good for the post office. I wondered about hers.

Tuesday's newspaper said the bandit made off with almost $60,000 and got clean away in a black vehicle (a black vehicle!) in spite of the roadblocks. Witnesses said they couldn't see much of his face with a hat pulled down around his ears. Didn't give much more of a description than that, except to say he looked kind of medium.

Tuesday afternoon I went straight from work to Piedmont, unexpected and uninvited, busting to report that license-plate scene I should have mentioned earlier.

Driscoll was at his desk with his reading glasses on, fountain pen in his hand, clearly preoccupied with the papers in front of him.

I barged in anyway, took a chair, and told him about it.

Driscoll glanced up and threw me a puzzled look. "What?" Now, this was not a *what* of surprise, more like one of not listening.

"That salesman was changing a license plate on a black Chevy in a deserted parking lot and it isn't license plate season. Don't you find that odd?" This time I got a bob of the head and the blank face that came with thought. "Couldn't it be related to the bank robbery? I mean, it was a black car, Driscoll."

"I suppose it could. Might also be a coincidence. We need to be wary of coincidences, Grace. They are the investigator's steel trap. We have been burned before when they masqueraded as fact."

"But don't you think we ought to report it?"

"Sure we should. I plan to drop in on Chief Eades in a day or two anyway, see what I can find out about his progress in the case. Cops always have more than they're willing to share with the newspapers. Actually, I welcome the opportunity to offer information. It's a good way to start, set a tone of cooperation." Driscoll leaned back and folded his arms across his chest. "Look, Grace, I can see you're excited about this. Maybe it's something, maybe it's not, but you need to concentrate on the matter at hand. Fact is, we can't move an inch without the name of that renter."

"You said to wait for the right moment and it hasn't come yet."

"Yes, I did say that. On the other hand, we can carry caution too far."

The next morning, thank goodness, my chance to sneak into the file came suddenly when I made it to work before grumpy Grace or Kenny or anyone else. Realizing this was it, my heart turned into a woodpecker. I chewed my gum like crazy and tried not to think, just marched to the drawer, opened it, rifled through the wooden box to number 45. Name on the card said Underwood. I slapped it up on the counter with one hand, grabbed for the camera with the other. Then it was just a matter of taking the picture, and I snapped an extra just to be sure. With shaky hands I put the card back in place, closed the drawer and walked away. Took half a minute or maybe less. Doubt if I ever breathed.

I spent the next few hours flying high and happy, relieved to have the job done at last and proud of the no-fuss result. Roberta kept looking at me and finally asked, "What's up with you? Is this your birthday?" I caught myself studying Kenny for signs of his suspicion, then decided Driscoll would find fault with such beginner behavior, which could draw suspicion itself.

After lunch I uncovered a third letter, but the sight had grown ordinary. Truth was, we just didn't need them anymore.

On the drugstore pay phone after work, I told Driscoll about the pictures and how smooth it went. He laughed out loud. Hadn't seen that before so I was left to imagine the sparkle that must have come with it.

"Did you notice the name and address on the card?" he asked.

"Not the address, but the name is Underwood."

"Good, okay, that's fine. Did you take more than one?"

"I took two. Should I get the film developed? I'm standing in a drugstore and they have a place right here."

"No, don't do that. In our business, we develop our own film."

"You do? I never heard of such a thing."

He chuckled. "We have a darkroom for that very purpose."

"Okay, I'll bring it to you, then."

"If you wouldn't mind."

If I wouldn't mind? Part of the job, I figured.

I drove over there and stayed only a minute, handed him the film canister with sudden concern for the contents. "What if they don't turn out?"

"Why look for trouble? We'll get enough of that anyway." He punched me playfully on the arm and glanced at the clock. "I have a meeting on another matter in ten minutes. Come on, I'll walk you to the door. The photographs will be ready later tonight. I'll give you a call."

After dinner, I carried a book into the parlor to be near the telephone. Around nine o'clock it let out two short rings. That meant us, so I answered.

"Your photographs look good," Driscoll said without a hello first. "The man's full name is Ralph Underwood and the address is in Stapleton. That's smart. He doesn't operate where he lives."

"Where's Bobby? Has he seen them?"

"Not yet. It's his wedding anniversary. Took his wife to the Regency Room, a swanky restaurant at the Roanoke Hotel. But he already said he's never heard of a man named Underwood. Tomorrow, the three of us will hop in the car and drive over there, maybe get a glimpse of this character, see if Bobby knows him by another name."

Eight

It rained most of Thursday. The sky cleared, though, by five in the afternoon for our trip to Stapleton. Driscoll took the wheel, Bobby beside him. I climbed in the back with a tangle of equipment—a large camera, binoculars, tripod, and I don't know what all.

Driscoll reached across the seat and handed me the photographs. The two of the lockbox form were clear and readable. Ralph Underwood. Yeah, he looks like a Ralph, I thought. The one of my shoes on the floor came out blurry but the other test shots looked fine. "What does Carpe Diem mean?" I asked.

Bobby said, "It's Latin for 'seize the day', which is exactly what we're doing."

We took the same roads I had taken … gosh, not even three weeks before, which started me thinking how much happened in that short amount of time, how lucky I was to spend the summer here rather than school, or Betula, or anywhere else.

In Stapleton, Driscoll found Erie Street, turned onto it and slowed to a crawl. "Okay, keep your eye out, we're looking for 720."

"There it is, that greenish one on the right," Bobby said.

Driscoll drifted just past the one-story house and pulled to the side.

"This is where the guy lives?" Bobby asked.

"Well, it's the address on the form, 720 Erie Street. Looks like it needs repairs."

"Yeah, and he wants me to pay for it, the dirty scum!" Bobby hit the seat with his fist.

"Dirty *rotten* scum," Driscoll added.

I wanted to call him a bad name, too, but couldn't come up with one.

Bobby ran a nervous hand through his hair. "I just want to know if I've seen the dirty rotten scum before."

"Okay, we'll sit and watch. Not here, though. Maybe back there." Driscoll nodded behind. He circled the block and stopped just short, in front of an empty lot with a construction trailer.

"I don't see a blue Plymouth," I said. "He must still be at work."

"Grace, what are the chances it's the same guy you saw? A thousand to one?"

"I don't know, but I'm telling you, it's him."

"How can you be so sure?"

"Sometimes, don't you just know things?"

Driscoll thought a moment. "Okay, hand me the camera." He set it beside him. "Now, reach me that blue box on the floor. Careful, it's heavy." He opened the box and removed a camera lens as long as my arm from wrist to elbow. He got the whole thing put together, aimed it at the house and took a few shots.

We saw a girl break out the front door at a run, about ten years old, my cousin Henry's age. Driscoll got shots of her bouncing a ball up the street.

A tired-looking woman came out with a broom and began to sweep the porch. More shots of that.

I glanced at my watch. We'd been waiting an hour. I wanted a bathroom but kept it to myself figuring the whole experience was part of the job.

Fifteen minutes later, the waiting paid off. A blue Plymouth drifted right by us and parked in front of the house.

"That's the car!" I declared in an excited whisper, no attempt to be humble. The man took his time getting out. When he opened the car door and stood out of it, he was even wearing the same plaid shirt. "That's him! That's the man I saw!"

"Well, I'll be damned," Driscoll said. Resting the weighty camera lens on the steering wheel, he began to click and kept on clicking until the man disappeared into the house. "Have you seen him before, Bobby?"

"No, thank goodness, never in my life."

"That does it for me, then. Like I said, it was nothing but a bluff!"

Bobby took a deep breath and let it out with a satisfied sigh. "Let's discuss the next step. First, I take my letter and show Whitney. Grace, have you met the postmaster?"

"Only for a minute."

"It's time to confess what you were really doing there."

"Will he be angry?"

"Miffed, maybe, but he'll understand."

"Whitney should be the one to contact the police," Driscoll said, "since Underwood has been committing mail fraud as well as blackmail."

"And what will the police do?" I asked.

"They'll arrest his stinking ass, that's what they'll do!" Bobby jerked his head around and grimaced. "Oh, excuse me, Grace."

I smiled at that. It reminded me of our police chief in Betula, Obie's dad, the way he cusses and then asks to be excused. "Does this mean my job is finished?"

"It'll be up to Whitney," Bobby said. "He might need you to stay until his injured employee returns. We don't want to leave him shorthanded." He peered over the seat at me. "I have another Latin phrase for you: Venimus, Vidimus, Vicimus."

"What does that one mean?"

"We came, we saw, we conquered. I think we're doing just that."

There was whispered talk at the post office Friday morning but not about me. They fired Grace Contee. It happened Thursday after Mr. Acres saw her slide a letter into her pocket. I know, I know. She did the same thing my first day and I never said a word, being new and all.

Well, right or wrong, I decided again not to say anything. And I kept mum, too, about finding her behind the lockbox wall. I mean, they had already fired her so what was the point. Evidently, the postmaster intended to do it anyway because of her bad attitude, waiting only for the return of the clerk with the broken wrist. But what grumpy Grace did with that letter on Thursday had forced his hand.

Then, during an inspection of her locker, Mr. Acres found more letters, a whole lunch bag full. They stretched over a thirteen-month period, all of them yet undelivered. Thirteen months, undelivered!

Up in the attic, putting away purses, Roberta draped an arm around me and whispered, "Want to know why you got that pigeonhole job? Grace Contee couldn't be trusted behind the wall, so they took it from her and gave it to you."

"Guess that explains her dislike for me. But what possessed her to hide those letters in the first place? That's what I want to know."

"I'll tell you what I think. It was jealousy, pure jealousy and meanness. I was up here when Mr. Acres found them in her locker. He emptied the bag on the table and, from what I could see, the letters were addressed to Grace's classmates, the popular ones. I was two years behind her in school, so I know."

Bobby showed up in the middle of the morning, went into the postmaster's office and closed the door, then came out a half hour later wearing a smile.

Two things came from the meeting.

First, about the blackmail letters and my involvement, the postmaster just shook his head and uttered, "Well, I'll be hanged," so he must not have been too miffed. He was apparently much more upset about those undelivered letters. The worst thing that could happen in a postmaster's world, he said. A shaming, awkward predicament caused by his own employee, he said. By comparison, the blackmail letters were merely an issue for the police.

And second, the woman who broke her wrist was returning to work in two weeks, which would free me up to leave then if I wanted. Didn't know how to feel about that. Truth was, as long as I could stay in Roanoke the rest of the summer, live in Maudie's boarding house and see something of Driscoll, I didn't much care about the rest.

Nine

For my Friday night date with Wesley, I rejected five outfits and then settled on a blue dress that came from Leggett's the day my car got hit.

The moment the doorbell rang, Bogart tore down the stairs barking. Miss Scott said, "hush, doggie," as she let her nephew in.

Not bad to look at, this Wesley Scott. Taller than me, which isn't saying much, I guess. White teeth in an easy smile, a razor-creased suit the same color as his sandy hair, a snowy shirt and even a bar for his tie.

In a shiny green Buick that looked brand new, he took me to the Regency Room at the Roanoke Hotel, the same place Bobby had taken his wife. The most expensive restaurant in town, according to Maudie. Polished cutlery on white linen, tables far apart, hovering waiters—that kind of place. Wesley was probably trying to impress me. I figured there were worse things a blind date could do.

We got situated at a table by a head man in a tuxedo. Then a waiter in a white jacket came about drinks. While we waited for them, Wesley was eager to tell me about himself and I was happy to listen. He had a lot to say, for example, on the subject of his new job—buyer for the men's department at Leggett's, which helped explain his picture-perfect look. It was a big promotion moneywise, he said, especially for someone his age, and it came with opportunity to travel. He had already been to New York City on the train to see the new fall line.

A different waiter showed up, dressed the same. They all appeared to be going to a dance. This one came to discuss dinner and took our orders without writing any of it down.

The interruption seemed to break Wesley's momentum, and he politely turned to ask about me. I quickly covered college and my summer at the post office. It was impossible to make the job sound interesting. I mean, leaving out my real purpose, there wasn't much of interest left to say. Now, this might not be accurate, but I believe Wesley sat there comparing my low mail clerk job to his high one, because what he did with his mouth seemed more like a smirk than a smile.

Then, over salads and an excellent crab dish, he described every detail of that trip to New York City. He even rapped out names of people he'd hob-knobbed with, looking across the table for my reaction. Not sure what he expected. I tried to appear impressed but I'd never heard of any of them, and wondered if what he said was mostly made up.

"This girl has never been to New York," I chimed in. "It would be fun to take the train there someday, just to go up in the Empire State Building."

"Oh, the Empire State Building! What a stirring sight, the tallest building in the world. The view from up there is magnificent!"

"You've been to the top? I'm envious."

"Well, I haven't been up there yet, but I plan to go, and it's what people say." He set his fork down on his empty plate and dabbed at his mouth with a napkin. "How about the Natural Bridge? Have you been there?"

"No," I said, feeling small from my lack of travel. Part of me wanted to tell him I *had* been there but it didn't seem important enough to waste a lie on. I took a quick glance at my wristwatch hoping he wouldn't notice.

"The Natural Bridge, another stirring sight, how something so immense could have been carved out simply by nature. They call it one of the seven natural wonders and it's only an hour from here."

"Oh, you've already been, then."

He cleared his throat and shifted in the chair. "Well, not yet, but that's what I've read."

Wesley was beginning to annoy me. It left the possibility of a relationship with him somewhat open to doubt.

He then fell into a description of his father's heroic service as a colonel during the war. I tried to show a face free of boredom but, honestly, he was telling me so much more than a person needed to know. Plus, Miss Scott had already told us about her brother's war service. It hadn't sounded quite so spectacular coming from her, and I believe she had said he was a lieutenant. I did not react, not with words anyway, but I bet my face said plenty.

I started to get sleepy, fought hard to stay awake and nearly yawned off twice. Couldn't resist another glance at my watch, and this time I didn't care so much whether he noticed.

"How about your father?" Wesley asked. "Was he in the war?"

"Uh, yes, he was in the infantry, European campaign." It was my dad's clipped answer when somebody pressed him about the war, an experience he wanted to forget.

"What was his rank?"

Now, why did he ask that? If this was a competition between fathers, he was on shaky ground with me. "Rank? He was a sergeant, I think, but what does it matter, Wesley? The war is over and he's a successful attorney now." Nobody gets away with treating my dad as anything but brilliant. I could have talked for hours about him and his good qualities. His wise advice, for instance, when he'd taught me not to brag.

I sat there stewing, my eye on the exit.

Wesley waved for the check and pulled out his wallet. "Do you like movies?" he asked, probably sensing our desperate need for a new topic.

"That depends," I mumbled. With somebody else, I would have loved going to a movie theater—one thing Betula did not have.

"From Here to Eternity is playing at the Rialto. It's a wonderful film, certainly deserving of all those academy awards."

"Then, you've already seen it."

"Well, no, but I plan to."

I let my anger slip out. "Now, wait a minute! If you haven't seen it, how do you know it's wonderful?"

"That's what people say. And it wouldn't have won all those awards otherwise, now, would it?" he said with a definite smirk.

On the drive back to the boarding house, Wesley described all the features of his new automobile—whitewall tires, leather seats and such. He said it cost $2250. No doubt about it, his Buick was a beauty. From somebody else, I wouldn't have minded a bit, but coming from him it grated on me and just sounded like another load of brag. I could have told him about my new Chevy and how I paid cash. Or my inheritance. I could have told him about that.

He knew I was angry but seemed to have no idea why. It just made the poor man try harder to impress me, which got me to wondering: Was I equally as ignorant about an annoying habit of mine?

Somehow, I made it to the end. When he pulled up in front of the boarding house, I made a quick reach for the door handle. "Well, thanks for the nice dinner, Wesley. It's getting late so I'll just let myself out."

"No, no, stay where you are. At least let me walk you to the door."

Nobody was waiting for us, except Bogart. I think we were both relieved, each of us feeling the failure.

"Thank you again for the delicious dinner," I said, just wanting to escape.

"You're welcome. At least that's one thing good about our evening."

The only thing, I thought, but did not say. He probably regretted choosing such an expensive restaurant. Wouldn't blame him if he did since the date was such a flop. I felt bad about the money but not enough to try again. And, surely he didn't think of me as a prize.

"Maybe we can go out again another time," he said.

"Maybe we can," I said, bobbing my head in agreement.

Neither of us meant a single word. I thanked him one more time and held out my hand for him to shake, hoping he would not try to kiss me. Then I made good my escape up the stairs with Bogart racing ahead.

Another moment with sticky-scene potential was breakfast the next morning. I considered skipping the meal altogether but knew I'd have to face Miss Scott sometime. "Well, how was your date last night," she asked.

The colonel had eaten earlier to prepare for the parade, so Maudie was the only other person at the table.

I offered the biggest smile I could muster. After all, it was not her fault. "Your nephew took me to the Regency Room, the fanciest restaurant I've ever been in, and we had a delicious meal." She stared at me with her mouth open, expecting more. When I didn't say anything else, she didn't either. She merely closed her mouth and glanced at Maudie, too much of a lady to pry. It was all true enough, what I said. If Wesley wanted her to know more, he could tell her.

When I came into the kitchen with breakfast dishes, Maudie asked, "Will you go out with Wesley again?"

"Once was enough," I said, frowning. "Had you met him?"

"Only for a minute. Seemed like a braggart to me, even in that short time."

"You might have warned me."

"Wouldn't dream of doing such a thing. It's not my place to interfere."

Ten

After breakfast, we all walked down to Campbell Avenue to claim good sidewalk space for Roanoke's Independence Day Parade. Turned out to be quite a spectacle for someone like me who had never seen a real parade before. While the sun beat down, high-kicking majorettes led the way flinging batons in the air and catching them with nary a fumble. A marching band of at least a hundred swept by us in red plumed hats.

Then came uniformed veterans from the wars. We caught the colonel's eye and he waved at us, proud as the winning piemaker at a fair. In full uniform with a chest full of medals, black horse dressed out in silver and leather, I must say he cut a fine figure.

On and on the parade went. Fire trucks and model-Ts, cowboys on horseback, and a float carrying Miss Roanoke in a white strapless gown. She waved to the crowd with a glove-covered hand, likely the only one on the street who was not in a sweat.

About those cowboys on horseback, one broke out of formation and sidled over to us. A splendid-looking man in a checkered shirt and cowboy hat, sitting high on a chestnut stallion.

Maudie obviously knew Vern Beckley and I wanted to know him, too. I mean, what woman would not want to know Vern Beckley—handsome and tan, deep blue eyes and dazzling smile.

While she made polite introductions, the horse seemed restless, pranced near the curb and bobbed its huge head. We all stepped back. It let out a whinny and Vern stroked the horse's neck. "Easy, boy, easy." He smiled down at me. "Excuse my horse. It's what he does at the sight of a pretty woman and when a twelve-hundred-pound animal with an independent mind acts this way there's not much you can do." Vern was obviously flirting with me.

Unfortunately, there was no time for anything more. He tipped his hat most charmingly and dashed to catch up with the others.

Maudie glanced my way and chuckled. "From that goofy grin, I'm betting you are interested in Vern Beckley."

"I certainly am."

She set her mouth in a frown and cut her eyes at me.

"Uh-oh, what does that mean? Is he married?"

She refused to say any more just then so I was left to wonder. But that didn't stop me from trying him on for size in my mind while a tractor float passed by. According to my eyesight and early reports in my head, Vern Beckley fit.

After the parade, back at the house, Maudie went straight to her apartment. I followed and stood in the open doorway of a sitting room done in flowery blues. "All right, what's the matter?"

She motioned me to a chair, removed her hat and hung it on a rack. "Grace, you know I don't like to meddle in other people's affairs…" I nodded and tried not to smile. "But I do have something to say about Vern Beckley. When it comes to him, I'm of two minds. On one hand, he's probably the greatest catch in the county. Family owns a cattle ranch, he could have anybody he wants. And he's the best kind of man, handsome and doesn't know it. On the other hand, he has taken up some serious drinking since he came back injured from Korea. At least, that's what I hear."

"Are you saying I shouldn't go out with him?"

"No, I'm not saying that. It isn't my place to tell you what to do. I'm only saying what I've heard. Plus, Vern can be quite a heartbreaker, you know, with those steamy blue eyes and all his qualities. A girl could get hurt."

"Well, it'll probably never come up, anyway."

"Oh, it'll come up."

"How do you mean?"

"Grace, you poor naive child, men are so easy to read. I spotted that look in his eyes when he saw you, and he knows you're here. Mark my words, you'll get your chance."

After that, I grew more interested in the ring of the telephone, felt too far away in my room and spent much of Sunday in the parlor or in the kitchen with Maudie. But she said I shouldn't be the one to answer a call from Vern Beckley. Might make me appear too eager. So we let Clarisse pick up on the three calls that day, all of them apparently for her.

Monday, I was back for another week at the post office. Nobody there seemed to know what had gone on with me. I bet they wondered when the police came about the blackmail matter and I got called into the postmaster's office to tell my side of things. But none of them asked me about it, not even Roberta.

71

At the Saturday meeting, Driscoll said the police searched Ralph Underwood's house and found lists of names. Bobby's name was on one of them. Three names had checkmarks. The poor schnooks who paid? Driscoll figured the man would be looking at three years in prison.

Bobby picked a donut out of a box on the table, took a bite and chewed. "I think the victims, all twenty-two of them, ought to be notified of the blackmail scheme, sort of as a public service. It could be done in a well-worded letter uncovering the crime, a simple clerical job."

"Nice idea," Driscoll said, "but who'd do it? Chief Eades is already stretched to the limit with the bank robbery and a new string of home break-ins he describes as baffling. And speaking of the bank robbery, the Chief *was* holding back information. The bandit wore gloves and passed a note to the bank teller that stated he had a gun. Nobody actually saw a gun but he kept a hand in his pocket as though he had one." Driscoll reached back, grabbed a folder off the desk and opened it in front of him. "Witnesses disagreed on the make of the getaway car, but a bank employee managed to get a partial license plate: 563-6 or 568-6. Couldn't say for sure whether the third digit was 3 or 8, and couldn't help with the last two digits at all. It was the best she could do peering through rain. The cops are busy checking Records for license plate matches, but that could take weeks."

"They need another Mrs. Penn," Bobby said. "She'd get the job done in a hurry."

"Why is it I never see Mrs. Penn?" I asked.

"Well, like now, you're here evenings or Saturdays and she doesn't work then," Driscoll said.

"Did you tell Chief Eades what I saw behind Piggly Wiggly?"

"I told him. He said he'd look into it. How long are you committed to the post office, by the way?"

"Through next Friday, the seventeenth."

"Do you want to stay longer?"

"Not particularly. They won't need me much after that."

"Well, you can work here with us the rest of the summer, if you want." Driscoll glanced at Bobby, who nodded agreement. "We're in desperate need of another pair of hands right now, Grace, I don't mind saying. On top of that, we promised Mrs. Penn a good, long vacation to visit her son in Chicago. But be warned … it's mostly a clerical job."

His words were music! Of course, I wanted to work with them and I didn't care if it meant clerical. Better that than pigeonholing all day without a purpose. And something else occurred to me: Who knew what the change might mean. At the very least it would mean working with Driscoll, learning from Driscoll, a chance to see him every day. I surprised myself with this strong reaction about a man too old for me.

Vern Beckley called Sunday afternoon. He sure took his time. It had been a week and a day since we'd met. From my room I heard the telephone's two short rings and tried not to wonder, but then my heart leaped when Maudie called my name up the stairs. Vern invited me out for Saturday night dinner. Maybe a walk around the lake afterward, he said. It sounded romantic, danged romantic.

On Monday after work I went to the Piedmont office at Driscoll's request. When I got there he was sitting at his desk behind a stack of folders. He grabbed one and joined me at the table. "Bobby will be here in a minute. He's already heard most of this."

Driscoll arched his back in a stretch, threw a long leg over the side of his chair and opened the folder.

"The police had a lucky break in their Records search. Turned up a plate number that could be a match to the partial plate. On top of that, it was reported stolen that Monday morning. The Chief seems certain it was used in the robbery." Driscoll raised an eyebrow at me.

I studied the floor as my spirits sank. "Certainly sounds likely. Then, it wasn't the salesman who robbed the bank. Gosh, and I was so sure."

"Well, hold on. The owner reported it *stolen* Monday but she couldn't say when it actually disappeared. She hadn't driven her car that whole weekend because she was sick with a cold."

"So, it could have been the license plate the salesman put on! Pretty good plan—use a dealer car from the lot, slap a stolen plate on it, rob a bank, then return the car and get rid of the plate."

"And one more thing. Actually, two things. Judging by what the bank teller described, Chief Eades believes the robber is left-handed."

"The car salesman is left-handed!"

"How do you know?"

"Well, he signed my papers with his left hand. Also, he had a tiny dab of toothpaste on the left side of his mouth."

"What does that prove?"

"That he brushes his teeth with his left hand."

Bobby walked in about then and took a seat beside me. "Never heard *that* before, and I'm in the business to notice things."

"Okay then, notice next time you brush your teeth. I bet you have toothpaste on your mouth where the toothbrush hit."

"Sounds reasonable to me," Driscoll said with a tease. "We'll call it the Dawson Toothpaste Theory and add it to our manual on investigation techniques."

"Do you think it's silly?"

"No, not at all." Driscoll reached over and jiggled my hand. "I'm joking with you, Gracie. You have keen observation skills. We respect that around here." He let go of my hand and tapped the scribbled notes in front of him. "The second thing … according to the bank teller, the man had a scar on his cheek." Driscoll looked at me, knowing I'd react.

"Now, wait a minute! The salesman has a scar on his cheek!"

"Yes, I remember."

"It was on his, uh . . ." I hesitated, picturing the salesman's face as we stood in the showroom, "it was on his right cheek, wasn't it? He did it! Doesn't this prove he robbed the bank?"

"Doesn't prove anything," Bobby said, "although the circumstantial evidence does seem to be piling up."

Friday, July 17 was my last day at the post office. They cut a cake and wished me well, a peach of a thing to do after only five weeks. Except for the postmaster, I had come into the job and then left it without anyone knowing what I did. There was something exciting about that.

On Driscoll's say-so and just to stay honest, I announced at the dinner table that my post office job had ended and I'd be working for Piedmont the rest of the summer.

"What will you do there, my dear?" the colonel asked politely.

"Oh, typing, filing, stuff like that. Maybe some research if I'm lucky." Truth was, I wanted another undercover job.

Eleven

No question this time about what to wear on a date. Only an elegant dress would do, and it had to be black. Saturday morning, I found one in a shop on Campbell Avenue, brought it home and stretched it across my bed. Maudie came up to see it, made me try it on and then whistled like a man. Clarisse stuck her head in the door, took one look and said it needed jewelry.

At five in the afternoon I began preparations for my date. It took every bit that long for bubble bath, nails, hair, and face.

Bogart picked up on the excitement, trailed after me from room to room, wondered what was going on. Sensing a reason to celebrate, he dragged out all his toys.

Promptly at seven, he abandoned those toys and flew down the stairs when the doorbell rang. Vern greeted Maudie in his lovely deep baritone, my cue to slide the new dress over my head and step into my best black shoes.

Vern gave me the once-over like I figured he would. He didn't whistle or even say anything, but I saw that look Maudie mentioned and took it as high praise.

As for his appearance, he'd shown up wearing clothes to catch my eye—leather boots and blue jeans on his long legs, under a well-worn suede jacket, shirt and tie. I happen to admire that sort of thing. It gave me pangs of sadness at the same time, though, because Obie often dressed that way.

In his pickup truck, Vern took me to the Log House, on a side street ten minutes away. No white tablecloths or carpet here. Checkered tablecloths and wide-plank floors were more the look. And, it was a seat-yourself kind of place. Vern chose a table near the bar and arranged us so he faced the entrance.

A waitress brought menus, nodded at me and said, "Evening, Vern."

"I see you've been here before," I said.

"Oh yeah, they know me. Best steaks in town."

He pushed his menu aside. "We'll order later but how about a drink? You're underage, I suppose."

I nodded. "Just Coca-Cola for me." I own stock in the company but it would have been bragging to mention it.

"Mind if I have something stronger?"

"Of course not."

He motioned to Dottie, the waitress. "A Coke for the lady and the usual for me."

"What's your usual?" I asked, nodding at his stubby glass when it came.

"Bourbon. Want some?" He held it out.

"No, thanks, I've already tried it. My dad drinks bourbon, except he likes his with ice." I regretted the remark immediately. Made me feel like a kid. Vern already seemed older, though he was only twenty-two. "Maudie told me you were in Korea."

"That's right, the infantry, until I got hit."

"Were you hurt bad?"

"Bad? No, I was the lucky one." He drained his glass and ordered another by raising a finger. "It was my best friend who got it bad. He stepped right on a landmine. Killed him and four others."

"That must have been horrible for you."

"Wasn't the best day, what I remember of it. All I got was shrapnel. Imbedded in four places, but nothing compared to them. The doctors there couldn't remove the one in my back. Too close to the spine, they said, so they flew me stateside and the docs in Richmond did the job. That was a year ago."

"Did they give you a Purple Heart?"

"Yeah, but I turned it down. Didn't deserve it for shrapnel, not when others were losing limbs and lives."

"My Uncle Charles got killed in Korea. He was in the Navy."

"Sorry to hear that. Were you two close?"

"No, I barely knew him. He fought in both wars so he was always gone."

"Two wars. Nobody wanted that except the men in it for a career. I served under a few of them."

"Do you have to go back in?"

"No, I'm done with the Army. Opens your eyes to the horrors in the world and I've seen enough." He brought the glass to his mouth with one hand and sliced through the air with the other. "Can't believe how naive I was then. I actually wanted to go, even after hearing war stories. In some ways, the war itself wasn't the worst. We traveled through the Port of Pusan, on the south coast of the Korean Peninsula. This was a real hellhole, a city full of refugees who had fled the North Korean invasion. Masses of homeless people living in despair wherever the eye turned." Vern took another drink, cleared his throat and coughed into his sleeve.

"But that wasn't the worst, either. We boarded a train going north to the war zone and there were orphans all along the tracks. Now, that was the worst, seeing those poor little kids, all alone. I'll never forget their pleading faces as long as I live. It was winter and they had congregated by the railroad tracks, freezing in cardboard boxes, living day to day by what they could steal to eat and wrap up in. Whenever the train stopped we gave them food, but the problem was just too big." He pointed a long finger at me. "I can tell you right now, every soldier on the train was concerned about those kids, but we had to turn away. That, or go crazy."

So, here was the reason he stood out as older. The things he had seen added years. I watched his glass go empty again. He'd already had two and this was before we even ordered dinner.

He had a scar on the back of his left hand. "What about this?" I asked, pointing.

"Yeah, that was part of it, another piece of shrapnel." He stretched his hand flat. It was a big hand, wider across than a dinner plate. The scar I guessed to be three inches long, more or less.

I reached out and gently touched it. Don't know why I did that but he seemed to like it, the way his eyes softened.

When Dottie returned with her little pad, Vern ordered steaks for both of us and tapped his glass for another drink. I ordered water for both of us wondering if Vern suffered partly from plain old thirst, the kind water was best for.

"Sorry, Grace, for goin' gloomy. We're supposed to be out for a good time. Here, let's drink to a better future and getting on with life." He held out his glass to clink with mine.

"Do you have a plan for getting on with life?" I asked.

"Yeah, I sure do. My family owns a beef cattle ranch, pure Angus. Not far from here, just south of Vinton. I've been working it since I recovered. It'll belong to me and my brother one day, and our goal is to double Dad's herd while he's still here." Vern saluted the idea with his glass.

"Coming from southwest Virginia I was surrounded by farms, but they were mostly dairy."

"Dairy is a different thing."

When Dottie brought the meals, I started right in on mine. Vern let his sit while he described the herd and the ways to expand it, the need to enlarge the barn and the other outbuildings. It all rang true to me.

"This will cost money, but I expect it to be a good cash source in the long run. The bank must agree because they just approved our loan. In four or five years you won't recognize the place." He ate a forkful of potato and some of his beans. "And I want to have kids of my own someday. I'll need a wife for that."

From the look on his face he was considering me.

"I can tell you one thing right now about my kids," he said, slapping the table. "They will always be safe and warm and well-fed. I'll see to that." He rolled his eyes, took a deep breath and let it out slow. "Sorry, Grace. There I go again."

"That's all right. You're passionate about it."

"Do you want children?" he asked.

"Sure I do, sometime." Frankly, children were way down on my list at nineteen. I felt even younger and started to question how good a fit I'd be for him. Soon, the only thing left on my plate was a bone. He seemed to be avoiding his steak altogether, as though cutting into it was just too much trouble. Sad to see him so interested in his glass, with a beautiful porterhouse in front of him.

"Tell me more about the ranch," I said, mostly to change the subject. "It's clear you like ranching."

"That's what I'm good at. I was practically born on a horse. Don't mean to brag, but I can shoot a fifty-cent piece right out of the air from the back of one."

Just like Obie.

Vern leaned across the table. He was going to say something serious. "There are three things most important to me in this world. Ranching, family, and ... I forgot the other one." He caught Dottie's attention and held up his empty glass. That would make four, and he had already turned dull of eye just in our brief time of sitting there.

"Maybe you've had enough to drink for now, Vern," I stuck my neck out to say.

He screwed up his face. "Is that what you're looking for, Grace, a man who doesn't drink? My brother doesn't drink. People act as though it's a wonderful thing, not drinking. Well, Hitler didn't drink, either. Consider that!"

It was the bourbon talking. It had left him nearly too numb to function. Paying the bill was a clumsy transaction and he leaned to the left on the walk to the door. He was drunk right down to his boot heels by then, unsteady enough that I linked my arm through his as a kind of anchor, and doubted the likelihood of a smooth ride home.

"Maybe I should drive us back, Vern, under the circumstances."

"Nah, that won't be necessary," he said, slurring his words. "I'll be fine in the night air."

Somebody opened the door, so all we had to do was walk through it to the porch. Turned out it was Driscoll who opened it, either him or Bobby, because they were both standing there.

Other People's Problems

Before I had a chance to speak up, Bobby said in the kindest of voices, "Vern, you look a bit ragged tonight. Driscoll will take Grace back and I'll drive you home in your truck. What do you say? We wouldn't want any accidents."

"Yeah, well, I guess you're right. Sorry about this, Grace. Maybe another time ..." He lifted his hand and seemed about to pat me on the head. I would have hated that. Instead, he bent down, tilted my chin, and we touched lips. Could hardly be called a kiss, which was probably a good thing with the others watching.

I thanked Driscoll three times on the walk to his car. The sun had dropped below the horizon so I couldn't read his face, but it had appeared pretty stormy in the porchlight. "How did this come about?" I asked.

"Maudie called. She was worried about Vern driving you home. Last summer, right on her street, a drunk teenager hit one of those big oak trees, the one with the gash in it. Killed himself and two friends."

"Gee, that's awful. Gotta admit, I was beginning to worry."

"Well, we feel responsible after bringing you here to work for us and all. Can't let anything happen to you until you're finished on the job." In the darkness I imagined the sparkle in his eyes that came with the tease in his voice.

Back at the boarding house, Maudie met us at the door with relief on her face. "You must come to Sunday dinner soon, Driscoll. We'll set a date when I'm not so sleepy," she said with a yawn.

In bed that night I couldn't stop thinking about Vern. It was the war driving him to drink, I knew that. Trying to drown in short glasses of bourbon that part he'd brought back home. It seemed odd and such a crying shame to watch a tall brave muscly man turn to jelly over something you can pour.

Twelve

Sunday morning found me staying late in bed to ponder my situation. After two blind dates, still nobody to take Obie's place, and I needed to be finished with him. Even if he changed his mind and wanted me back, I couldn't trust him. Fact was, the man I trusted most besides my father was Driscoll.

I know, I know, too young for him, but that hadn't stopped me from trying him on for size once a week. He fit pretty well, unfortunately. And it hadn't stopped me from wanting to slide over on the ride home and link an arm through his, like I used to do with Obie. Of course, I didn't let myself do anything more than shift the tiniest bit, enough to satisfy the urge without having him notice. Such a bold move had to be his idea and there was no more chance of that than a blizzard. Driscoll was not my boyfriend, for goodness sakes, he was my boss, and nine years older. But that didn't cause me to abandon all hope. I kicked off the covers and stretched like a contented cat at the thought of my new job.

Back in June, Driscoll had said there were five investigators at Piedmont. So far, I had not met the others or seen much of Eleanor Penn, the office manager, who had left for a vacation.

Driscoll set me up with a desk in their reference room, apparently the only unoccupied space left. It was nice in there, had a window with a view of the lawn, and only two doors down the hall from Driscoll's. It reminded me of my father's in a way, small and rectangular in shape, one long wall taken up entirely by bookshelves, and a mimeograph machine in the corner. I studied their crowded shelves, curious to see the kind of reference books these investigators think important enough to keep. Some looked familiar—the United States Code, volume of the Virginia State Statutes, collection of leather-bound law books like my dad's, though maybe a little less thumbed through. There were also volumes on local statutes, thick files on Piedmont's previous cases, and a few on high-profile national cases that must have been interesting to them. These files, bulging with newspaper clippings, were held together by rubber bands.

I got called into a meeting almost the first thing. Morning meetings like this were routine, I found out, and they were now going to include me. We discussed my first assignment, which was to send out letters to those twenty-two blackmail victims. Driscoll and Bobby had already decided what the letters ought to say. They told me to use the company letterhead to add a touch of authority and mail them in envelopes with Piedmont's return address. Here's the body of one:

Dear Blackmail Victim,

  You will be happy to hear that the threatening letter you received recently from an unnamed source was an attempt at blackmail, the threats unfounded. The man who sent your letter, and twenty-one others just like it, has been arrested, awaiting trial on two felonies—attempted blackmail and mail fraud.

They had a small disagreement about the salutation. Bobby wanted to use the person's name. Driscoll preferred "Dear Blackmail Victim" because it spelled out the truth from the start. I sided with Driscoll. His way would allow me to type a perfect letter only once and then make copies with the mimeograph machine. I could have the letters finished by the end of the day. Bobby liked the sound of that and soon gave in.

The biggest job was addressing the twenty-two envelopes. They all went to men, by the way. Were women less likely to be guilty of something? Ralph Underwood must have thought so. I wondered if it was true.

As the week went on, my two guys busied me with more typing and filing, but that was okay. And I met the other investigators when they came into the reference room. One of them gave me a three-page letter to type, and that was okay, too.

The following Wednesday afternoon, Driscoll stuck his head in and motioned me to Bobby's office. Bobby was seated at the table with a man I hadn't met.

"Grace, this is Mr. Gridley," Bobby said as I took a chair. "He received one of our letters and is about to tell us why he's here."

"Call me John," the man said, glancing around. "I'm here to see that this blackmailer gets punished. Do you need any witnesses? I want to help."

"I know how you feel," Bobby said. "I got one, too."

"You married?"

"Yes, I am."

"Did your wife see the note?"

"No, thank goodness."

"You were lucky. I was out on the road when mine came in the mail. Never even knew about it. My wife read it and sent the money. Why did she do that? Because she believed it. Caught me with another woman five years ago and assumed I was at it again. I wasn't, just for the record, but I might as well have been. That blackmail note caused her to see a divorce lawyer. I didn't know any of this until we got your letter. She told me everything, then."

"Will she call off the lawyer now?" Bobby asked.

"She's still pretty upset after stewing on it for weeks, so we'll see. I knew something was wrong the minute I got back home, but she wouldn't tell me what." He leaned toward Bobby. "You know how that is."

"I hope it helps in the end, learning about all those other notes sent out."

"It will, if anything can. Without your letter, I wouldn't stand a chance." Mr. Gridley made a move to leave. "I just wanted to thank you all in person and offer my help."

Bobby walked him to the lobby and then came right back. Driscoll and I were still sitting there.

"I am damned lucky Jane didn't read my letter. She often gets to the mail before I do but sets aside the envelopes addressed only to me. If she had read it, I would have been caught off my guard, unable to hide my guilt, might even have confessed. Then, I'd be the one dealing with a divorce lawyer."

On the inside, I completely agreed with his wife's likely reaction. On the outside, all I did was give Bobby a sympathetic nod.

"Jane can forgive me many things—drinking milk straight from the bottle, scratching my back with a fork—but never an affair."

"You scratch your back with a fork?" I blurted.

A day or two later, Driscoll gave us another update from the police. "Chief Eades now apparently has three persons of interest."

I smiled at the phrase, "persons of interest," something only a cop would say.

"The first is the car salesman, based on your tip, Grace. They questioned Norm Nelson and he denied everything, of course. It wasn't him putting a license plate on a car, he did not rob the bank, etc. The Chief is still interested, but the only evidence is the scar on the guy's cheek, and that's not enough. The second person is the woman with the stolen license plate."

"Why is she on the list?" I asked.

"Could be in on it with somebody, maybe a boyfriend. She reports the plate stolen, he uses it to rob the bank. If a witness remembers the number, it'll just lead back to a stolen plate."

"It's happened before," Bobby said.

"And the third came from the Records search, another possible match to the partial plate, and this one was on a black Ford Mainline. The Chief thinks this guy, Stewart Osten, is a good bet. He lied about where he was that day. Says he was on the job at Sperry Office Equipment but the time sheets don't bear him out. And listen to this. He, too, has a scar on his cheek. How likely is that?"

"Damned unlikely and a real shame," Bobby said. "A scar can usually narrow a list down to one suspect. Well, friends, we just entered coincidence territory."

I sat there in silent frustration as the car salesman lost favor. Sometimes, you just know things, and I was pretty sure he robbed the bank.

Thirteen

When they brought Stewart Osten in for questioning, he could not come up with an alibi. I found that odd. He'd had time enough to grow one. Why hadn't he? I mean, even the guilty offer alibis.

The police searched his house, car, office. I figured they wouldn't find anything, and they didn't. But he got charged with the bank robbery just the same.

His arraignment was set for the following day and Driscoll agreed to take me. Our drive to the Salem Courthouse was surprisingly silent until I broke it. "Driscoll, I just realized it's been over a month since the robbery."

"Not so very long with a crime like this."

"Yeah, but will Piedmont get involved if the police don't recover the money?"

"Indeed, we will. Shenandoah Life and Casualty insured Salem Union Bank and we work for Shenandoah. We're a long way from that, however."

"I still think they arrested the wrong man."

"I know you do, but we can't push the point any further. We'll just have to believe that the truth will win out. In the meantime, we want to be careful with the police. We won't interfere, we won't ask questions beyond our involvement, and if we have something they need we give it to them. Chief Eades already understands we'll take over if he fails."

"Do you know the suspect's attorney?"

"James Trask, good man."

"He'll need to be good with no alibi to work with. Don't you think it's strange that the guy has done so little to defend himself?"

"Well, Grace, it could be that he's guilty."

Driscoll and I found seats in the back gallery, surrounded by others who'd come to observe. We would sit through six arraignments before Stewart Osten's turn. In each case, the one in trouble stood before the judge, sometimes with a lawyer, sometimes not. The prosecuting attorney was always involved, a tall thin man in a too-big suit. I paid particular attention when he talked, since prosecution is my goal, but voices didn't carry back to the gallery that well. Those six arraignments were quick, pretty much the same, and the judge granted bail in all of them.

Then, a court officer brought a handcuffed Stewart Osten in through the side door. Anybody could tell he was in more trouble than the rest, yet his business still only took five minutes. James Trask appeared from somewhere and of course the prosecutor was there.

I had to listen hard to hear what all got said. The judge's voice rang clear enough, perched on a platform the way he was. "Mr. Osten, you've been charged with bank robbery with a firearm. It is a federal crime that can carry with it a sentence of up to 45 years in a federal penitentiary. How do you plead?"

Trask, speaking for his client in a voice barely hearable, pled not guilty.

Driscoll had already told me bail wasn't possible, this being a federal crime. Trask asked for it anyway, which got a rise out of the prosecutor. The lawyers bantered back and forth until the judge called a halt and settled it. "The defendant is to be remanded in the county jail."

It was all very interesting to me, this early stage of jurisprudence. But even so, my mind kept drifting somewhere else. From the moment he appeared, I knew I'd seen Stewart Osten before. We even spoke once. It was at Stapleton College while I worked afternoons in President Beard's office. He had rushed in lugging his heavy toolbox, rain dripping off his hat, to repair our ailing mimeograph machine. We laughed about the freakish hailstorm I'd been witnessing out the window and he had just run through. There in the courtroom, I shamefully remembered thinking of him as handsome, how I looked for and found a ring on his finger, but still pictured myself with him in a, well, you know how I do. I had seen him another time, too, or maybe twice, at Lake Lorraine with his family—a pretty blonde wife and a baby old enough to crawl. They were picnicking on a blanket under a big oak tree, off to themselves.

I glanced around expecting to find her in the gallery with us, knowing her husband was innocent and tortured by the goings on. She wasn't, and I didn't blame her.

As the suspect left the courtroom through that same side door, he looked back our way with sadness and pain. My eyes followed his and landed on a dark-haired woman who gave him a brave smile and a nod, then collapsed into tears when the door banged shut. I froze in the moment, ceased all observing, even stopped chewing my gum. Wasn't sure what to make of the scenes I had witnessed but, together, they couldn't add up to good.

Driscoll saw me staring at her. "That must be his wife," he whispered.

I gave him a doubting look. "We need to talk."

Reporters had been banned from the courthouse, waiting outside. We weaved our way through.

Back in the car, I told Driscoll about the blonde and the baby. "I'm afraid she must be a girlfriend on the side. I mean, they acted too chummy for anything else."

Driscoll gawked at me. "Are you sure about this?"

"About what I saw, yes. What it means, I'm only guessing. Do you think his attorney knows about her?"

"I doubt it."

Driscoll decided right then to head back to the courthouse and find James Trask.

"Well, I'll be damned," Trask said at the news. It was hard to tell whether he was more relieved or annoyed. "This might explain why he has refused to give an alibi, but if that's the reason, my client is a damn fool."

"What are you going to do?" Driscoll asked.

"He's still in the courthouse. I'm going to go wring his neck. You two come with me."

We were seated at a table in a small conferring room when a guard brought in Stewart Osten. Clearly, he recognized me. It was plain on his face. That, and mounting fear.

Trask confronted him immediately. "This young woman says she saw you at Lake Lorraine with a blond woman and a baby. Care to explain?"

The prisoner looked down at his handcuffs. Driscoll and I just sat there. It was Trask's show. He pounded the table in frustration. "Talk to me, Stewart! Are they the reason you won't give an alibi? Were you with them that day? I don't think you appreciate the gravity of your situation. You're about to spend the balance of your life in a federal prison, all to cover an affair."

Can't say for sure that I caused it, but he all at once caved from the pressure and confessed the whole thing. "It's not an affair. She's my wife, and that baby is my daughter."

Nobody said a word. In the stillness I could hear distant sirens out the window and a ringing telephone down the hall.

Trask rubbed his face with both hands. "Hell fire, boy, how did you get into such a predicament?"

Stewart coughed and then cleared his throat. "I'm honestly not sure, exactly. Somehow, it just happened. I love both of them. It's possible, you know, to love two women at the same time. And I love that baby," he said, wiping at tears. "I would gladly go to prison if it would keep them from getting hurt."

"Well, it's all going to come out now. It's my job to save you from yourself. Do they know about each other?"

"Audrey doesn't know a thing and she's going to fall apart. Sarah, she knows. I told her a week ago."

"Can she, will she, provide you with an alibi?"

"Yes, but ... must she?"

Trask dismissed his client with a look and turned to us. "I'll pay her a visit this afternoon. It might be a good idea to have you two go with me."

"It's all such a horrible mess," Stewart said. "In truth, forty-five years in prison doesn't seem so bad."

The guard took Stewart away.

"Well, this is a surprising turn of events," Trask said in the hall. "My client has you to thank, Grace. The man has no idea what his life would have been like. He's guilty of bigamy, not bank robbery. Now, bigamy is a crime in the Commonwealth of Virginia, he'll still need to answer for that. But at least it isn't federal. At least his time served will be measured by weeks in jail, not decades in prison."

In Trask's car on the way, news of the arraignment was all over the radio—a not-guilty plea from the prime suspect in the bank robbery, and the denial of bail.

Sarah opened the door to Trask's knock and the three of us took in the scene: her red-stained eyes and overused handkerchief, radio playing in another room, baby toddling around.

She motioned for us to sit down. "I heard what happened on the news," she said, dabbing at a fresh round of tears. "They're reporting it over and over. They even gave his name. Can they do that?"

"Sure, they can," Trask said. "He's out there now, he's been charged. Stewart is in serious trouble. He'll go to prison for a long, long time unless he comes up with an ironclad alibi. And that's what we're here to talk about. We have one burning question—whether he was with you the time of the bank robbery, Monday afternoon, June 29."

Sarah nodded in a guilty, embarrassed sort of way.

"Are you sure?"

"Yes, we heard the news of it together on the radio."

"Are you willing to testify to that, despite what he's done to you?"

"Will I have to go to court?"

"Not open court, no, but for the prosecutor to drop the charges, you'll need to give a sworn statement in person."

Stewart Osten's picture was on the front page of Friday's newspaper but the story behind it was already old news.

Trask said Sarah's misery was still so pitifully raw that the prosecutor believed her without any doubts. He dropped the charges and released Stewart from jail that same afternoon.

I call this a fitting turn of events for an innocent man. To the police, however, it meant they were still stuck with an unsolved bank heist and $60,000 in missing cash.

The Saturday newspaper reported on Stewart's release. Not with as big a splash, but that was because reporters never heard about the second wife. Maudie and the others had a lot to say about it at breakfast. Me? I could not say a word.

Fourteen

Sunday was going to be a hot one. I could feel it already. In bed half-awake, twisted in too many covers, I felt that sure heat of the day. I felt it even without the covers, and rolling to a cooler place. Made me wonder if it was merely the summer heat I felt, or a subtle blanket of dread.

Lying there, I thought of Driscoll and remembered he was due for dinner, which chased all the dread away. It popped me right out of bed, in fact, and I hit the floor thinking of clothes. About the time Bogart came scratching, I had settled on a favorite yellow sundress.

Early in the afternoon, when I volunteered to set the table, Maudie smiled and let me do it, no longer bothered by a lodger's help on a Sunday. She told me to use the best china and put Driscoll in the vacant place at the end, where Dad sat a few weeks before. It was within striking distance of Clarisse and I didn't like it, but there was nothing to be done.

Out front, an hour or so before dinner, a man and his dog got hit by a car. We heard the screech of tires and all the commotion from the kitchen. Maudie called the police and we ran outside. The man was hurt but still alive. We weren't so sure about the poor little dog.

The driver was already out of his car, bent over the man. "They ran right out in front of me! First, the dog and then the man chasing after it. I swerved but ..." He began to pace back and forth in a panic, hands over his face in despair.

We soon heard sirens bearing down. They drew a crowd. Two officers pulled up in a squad car and screeched to a stop. Then, two more. And then, an ambulance. Attendants stooped down to work on the man, packing him off to the hospital.

The driver was a candidate for the hospital, too, seemed to me. Had a knot on his forehead the size of an egg, probably from the steering wheel. Couldn't have been his fault, as much a victim in this as the man and the dog. And he obviously felt bad, repeating "I'm so sorry" over and over at the sight of that dog lying limp in the road.

Maudie and I gave the man a glass of water and covered the dog with a towel. She went back in the house to check on dinner as Chief Eades rolled in to study the scene.

In my yellow sundress and sandals I stayed in the yard and leaned against a tree, close enough to watch but far enough away not to intrude. The officers taking photographs and measurements did not seem to mind my being there. In fact, I saw them stealing quick glances at me and took it as a form of flattery.

Chief Eades showed interest in whether the man had been drinking. "Is he inebriated?" he asked. Inebriated. Now, that's a word you don't hear very often. I think it's a police word. The only other person ever to use it in my hearing is Chief Sayer in Betula.

Clarisse came out on the porch in a scoop-necked dress and high heels, earrings glittering on the sides of her head, blond hair piled up perfectly. I can do something similar with my hair but it takes me a long time. As she stood there shielding her eyes from the sun, the flattering glances shifted from me to her and how well she filled out that dress. All at once I felt dowdy and flat as a plank.

Driscoll showed up about that time for dinner, boyish and adorable in a loose tie and straw hat, clearly surprised by the commotion.

He smiled over at me (which made me feel better) and then got off to the side with Chief Eades, who kept wiping sweat off his forehead with a handkerchief.

I stayed out there until the scene cleared and the chief drove away, but so did Clarisse. When Driscoll and I walked up the porch steps together, she greeted him with one of those sparkly smiles of hers. Then she stepped in close enough to encourage hugging and he gave her one. I didn't know it then, but that little encounter was only the beginning. I got to watch Clarisse operate at her best all afternoon.

Maudie served chicken-fried steak for dinner. In case you don't know, it's ribeye steak floured and fried just like chicken, and it's just as big a mess to prepare.

I saw all that mess helping her carry full platters into the dining room. And I saw her wipe gravy off her glasses with her apron just before walking through. It had become a familiar sight and always made me smile.

The moment we sat down, Clarisse started in on Driscoll. By the time the platters had been passed, it was all very clear: Clarisse's attention would be aimed at him, and the Colonel was to be kicked to the side like an old combat boot. She took up her napkin and smoothed it across her lap. "I saw you talking to Chief Eades out there. Are you friends with him?"

"Not friends, exactly, no, but we get along. It's important to get along with the police in my line of work."

"Insurance investigations. Wasn't it just a few months ago that your company was in the newspapers for recovering the cash in an old bank robbery?"

"Yes, the Bunker Andrews robbery."

I wanted to speak up, say I had been involved, too, but it would have been wrong, and a brag. Besides, Driscoll was reminding me to say nothing by deliberately not looking my way.

"And another time, too, recently. Something about a diamond necklace ..."

"Yes, the owner filed a fraudulent claim, said the necklace had been stolen when it hadn't. Shenandoah Life and Casualty Company, a client of ours, was the insurer in both cases."

"And, you found the necklace?" Clarisse leaned over and put a hand on his wrist. "Very impressive. You are obviously good at your job."

I wanted to slap her.

Driscoll squirmed in his seat. "Yeah, well, it was an easy find. The man had given it to another woman. When his wife discovered it missing, he pretended it was stolen and filed a claim."

Maudie shook her head and chimed in, "I don't know which is worse, giving his wife's diamond necklace to a girlfriend or filing a false claim."

The colonel looked up from his mashed potatoes and mumbled through a mouthful, "The fraudulent claim was worse."

"That's right," Driscoll said. "From a legal standpoint the fraudulent claim was worse, a felony. It was no crime at all for him to give away a necklace he had purchased."

Clarisse's gaze flickered to the colonel and then back to Driscoll. Miss Scott sat there quietly, shifting her eyes from person to person, content only to listen. I was not content to listen but that's what I did, just sat there like a lump and picked at my food. Frankly, I couldn't think of a single thing to say. Clarisse was leading by way of her questions, as though we were playing a card game and she had the trump. Maudie kicked me under the table with amusement on her face, seeing Clarisse as a game-player, too. It helped a little bit, I guess.

Clarisse placed a finger across her smiling mouth. "What about this recent bank robbery? Who insured Salem Union?"

"Shenandoah. Around here, they get most of the bank business, insuring against losses such as this."

"The police just lost their only suspect. What happens if the money isn't recovered? Will the case be yours?"

"The police still own it, still have plenty of time, and Stewart Osten was not their only suspect. But, yes, if they don't recover the money, Shenandoah will call us in, and they'll pay us handsomely to find it. Better our substantial fee than the $60,000 bank payout."

"What is your substantial fee, if you don't mind my asking." She sat there, eyes alert and a bit too round, impatient for the answer.

"Fifteen percent of the amount recovered."

Humph, I already knew that. Actually, I knew most of what Driscoll said, except the part about the diamond necklace. First I'd heard of that.

"And what do the police think when you're called in?" Clarisse asked. "They probably resent it."

"Understandably, they do. But we encourage working together and avoid showing them up to be wrong. Can't afford to get too cocky because we might fail, too. We failed flat with the Bunker Andrews heist, and Shenandoah had to make good on a $40,000 claim. Three years later we finally did recover the cash, but only because of a tip that came out of the blue from a surprising source."

"That's interesting! What kind of a tip, and from whom?"

"Afraid I can't tell you that, Clarisse."

Driscoll smiled directly at me that time and I smiled back.

"How did you get into this line of work?" Clarisse then asked.

Was there no end to her questions?

"The Army, during the war. Right out of basic training I was assigned to the intelligence-gathering staff of my battalion. It suited me just fine, and Bobby, too. That's how we met. After the war, our commanding officer, Major Curtis Brenner, founded Piedmont Investigations, hired us, and here we are."

Well, darn! I certainly did not know that!

In the gap between dinner and dessert, Clarice pulled out a lighter, a Zippo like Obie's, and set it on the table. Then she found a cigarette, held it between her lips with two fingers and looked expectantly at Driscoll to light it. He did. This gave her an excuse, by way of a thank you, to reach over and caress the top of his hand.

Maybe it was my imagination or wishful thinking but he looked uncomfortable to me. He squirmed again, this time more obviously, shifting in his chair the tiniest bit away. Maudie looked straight at me and blinked. She'd noticed, too.

The cigarette added to Clarisse's sophistication, I must admit. The way she held it in the air just so when she wasn't puffing, in order to show off her red lacquered fingernails. Made me want to take up the smoking habit myself and make a trip to Fletcher's for my own nail polish.

After an Apple Crunch dessert, the colonel and Miss Scott soon retired upstairs. Clarisse stood up from her chair and said to Driscoll, "Let's go sit on the porch. It's cooler out there and they need to clean up here." She might as well have called Maudie and me the "hired help" with a comment like that.

Driscoll glanced briefly at me and then went.

We made fast work of clearing the table, left the mess for later and joined them on the porch as though Driscoll needed protection, and maybe he did.

Clarisse had moved to politics and the president and the booming economy by then, fascinated by all of Driscoll's opinions. Meanwhile, Maudie covered her frequent yawns, and my mounting resentment got harder to hide.

When Clarisse asked where the best place would be to park her money long-term, Driscoll flatly said he didn't know. I guess he'd finally had enough, or maybe he'd picked up on Maudie's need for a nap. He glanced at his watch and stood up to leave. Then, bless his heart, he made a point of looking directly at me. "Grace, I'll see you at the office in the morning. Actually, walk me to my car if you wouldn't mind. I have a little something to discuss."

Turned out, he didn't have anything to discuss. I think he did that just to push me and everybody else back where we belong.

Into the evening, I analyzed the time at the table and brooded about it. Clarisse had asked Driscoll some interesting questions, ones I'd never once thought to ask. She was really quite good. On top of my jealousy, I had to admire her expert handling of men. As the sun disappeared behind the trees, I went looking for Maudie and found her wrapped in a robe in the kitchen.

She was slicing a beautiful summer tomato and smiled tolerantly at me. "Want a snack? You didn't eat much at dinner. A tomato sandwich, say, with plenty of mayonnaise." She made us both one using leftover rolls. "Chocolate milk would be good with this. Why don't you pour us each a nice cold glass."

We sat at the kitchen table to eat.

"You seem low," she said. "It's Clarisse, isn't it? The way she behaved with Driscoll."

All I did was shrug, surprised, I must say, by how much Clarisse had bothered me.

"I'll tell you what I think. Ray Driscoll appeals to you."

Maudie wanted a reply but I didn't have one.

"Well, you needn't worry about Clarisse. She's had her chance."

"Yeah, but I have watched Clarisse the last few weeks, the way she treats the colonel. He's a different man, a younger man, when she's around. I didn't like it one bit when she tried the same thing with my father, and I got mad enough to drown puppies today. But it was plain old jealousy, too. Fact is, I ought to take lessons from her."

"What kind of lessons? How to play a man?"

"How to *treat* a man, more like."

"A kinder word, but what's the difference? Is she sincere? And what has it gotten her besides a bad marriage and steady alimony coming in."

"While we're on the subject of Clarisse, I saw her out on Columbia Avenue the other day with a cigarette in her hand. In Betula, women aren't supposed to smoke on the street." To be truthful, this statement satisfied the mean side of me. I figured it would set Maudie off, and it did.

"I could say something here but I don't like to gossip." She took the last bite of her sandwich, chewed a long time and then made a big deal out of wiping her mouth. "Except, Roanoke women aren't supposed to smoke on the street, either. It's just not ladylike. If you ask me, Clarisse pushes against all the boundaries of feminine decorum, which is what rankles me most about her."

"Interesting that Clarisse and Bogart don't like each other. I noticed it right off."

"Yeah, well, I have always viewed my dog as a pretty good judge of character, and that's all I'll say."

Fifteen

At the meeting the next morning, Bobby asked about dinner. Driscoll simply said, "It was delicious. Always a pleasure to eat at Maudie's table." Those were his only words on the subject of Sunday.

"Well, I learned something at dinner," I said, "about your commanding officer. Never even heard of Major Curtis Brenner until yesterday."

"Curtis is no longer a major," Bobby said, "but he is certainly still the boss. You haven't heard about him because he's been away since April, on assignment in New York."

"New York? If you don't mind me asking, how did an investigator from Roanoke get an assignment in New York?"

"Curtis has contacts in CIA, from his years in the military and after. The assignment came from there."

Driscoll rapped a pencil on the folder in front of him. "Thank you, Bobby, nicely done. You've led us right to the first item on the agenda. A new job is about to pop, filtering down through that same CIA channel. Nothing definite yet but sounds like a small undercover job and there might be a spot in it for you, Grace, if you're interested."

"An undercover job from the Central Intelligence Agency?" I tried to appear unruffled by such news. "But when does it begin? School starts September eighth."

Driscoll turned to a calendar on the wall. "That's more than a month away. We expect details by the end of this week and they're hoping for a quick result."

"Don't get too excited," Bobby said. "It'll mean many hours of just watching out a window."

"I don't care! Is it here in Roanoke?"

Driscoll held up a hand. "More on that later. Let's move on. The second item also involves you, Grace. Chief Eades is looking at your car salesman again, this time with a more devoted eye. He's sending an officer out to get a signed statement on that license-plate incident you witnessed." Driscoll glanced at his watch. "He should be here in an hour."

When the police officer arrived, he obviously knew my Piedmont boys. The three of them at first talked baseball — whether the Brooklyn Dodgers would make it to the World Series like the year before, and whether they had any chance of a win against the Yankees.

After that, the officer turned to me and listened with big round eyes to my brief account. Then he asked me to write out a statement and sign it.

Here's what I wrote:

> I, Grace Dawson, saw Chevy car salesman, Norm Nelson, put a license plate on a black Chevy behind the deserted Piggly Wiggly on Sunday afternoon, June 28.

I know, I know. It's an awfully short statement. By the officer's expression it might have been the shortest he'd seen. "Is that enough?" I asked nervously. "Anything more would be my own conclusions. Right? I mean, the whole thing seems odd, don't you think?"

The officer smiled and nodded. "Will you be a willing witness to this statement in court?"

"Yes, by golly, a most willing witness, since he's the one who robbed that bank the next day."

The police followed Norm Nelson for over a week. They searched all the places they could think of where he might have hidden $60,000. The effort gave them nothing. We, Driscoll and I, were not surprised. The $40,000 from the Bunker Andrews robbery in 1949 had been hidden in the basement of an abandoned, burnt-out house. It would never have been found without the tip from my college roommate, but that's another story.

Finally, with no leads left to pursue, and believing him guilty, Chief Eades called Norm Nelson in to try a sneaky old trick. I wish I had been there to see it, but at least Driscoll saw it and told Bobby and me.

A policeman apparently sat Nelson in a stuffy room and left him sweating in there for thirty minutes before the Chief came in. The conversation went something like this:

The Chief said, "Well, Nelson, I called you in merely to tie up a few loose ends, but I just had the most incredible luck. Cops brought a guy in this morning on a charge of breaking and entering. He's a career criminal, claims to know where the bank heist money is hidden, says he'll give it up in exchange for a deal. They're working on that deal upstairs. Might take a day or two but I think he'll lead us right to it. Pure, dumb luck, really."

"Why tell me?" Nelson said, "I had nothing to do with that robbery."

"A guy with brains would confess to it now, cut his own better deal."

"I tell you again, I had nothing to do with it! Besides, finding the money isn't the same as proving who took it."

"True. Although, the FBI can lift fingerprints off bank bags now. They do it all the time. What a marvelous modern world we live in, hey?"

Driscoll said the chief put on a fine act, delivering it all with a perfect mix of certainty and indifference. Then he assigned four officers to shadow Norm Nelson, watch his every move in a kind of leapfrog fashion to avoid notice. They didn't need to do it for long.

That very night, Norm led them right to the loot, stuffed under the seat of a rusted-out car in a field halfway to Blacksburg. I can only imagine the difficult choice it must have been for him—whether to play it cool and stay away, or take a chance and move it. He chose wrong. Driscoll said people like him usually do.

About Stewart Osten, he still has a bigamy charge to answer to, which is a misdemeanor in the Commonwealth of Virginia. Driscoll says he might still get jail time but it'll be for a whole lot less. Until then he's staying in a roadside motel.

His wife, Audrey, is already on her way to a divorce. With no children, it's an easy decision for her.

The other wife, Sarah, needs no divorce since her marriage was never valid. I guess she hadn't realized that, and hearing it just piled anger on top of hurt. "I want to get rid of him," she told me, "just push him right out of my life!"

I bet she'd do it, too, if she didn't have that baby to think about.

Stewart said he wants to marry Sarah when the divorce comes through. He told Driscoll that. "For real this time," he said, "and be a daddy to the little girl."

Well, he has some fence-mending to do in that department. Part of me wants to interfere, help him mend that fence. My father has always urged me to stay out of other folks' business. I could hear him say it again.

When Driscoll called a meeting about that undercover job, he started by saying I wasn't locked in, I could still decline after hearing the details. Made me wonder if he knew me at all.

"We've been hired to watch a house on 272 Willow Drive. Not far away, only about ten minutes. This is it." Driscoll slid a photograph of a boxy two-story across the table. "CIA is searching for a married couple who fled northern Virginia a month ago and disappeared. They might be living here. One of three possible locations, apparently. The agency is setting up watches on the others as well. They know a man and woman are living in this house. Our job is to first determine, through observation and camera work, whether it's the couple they're looking for. If it isn't, our work will be done, probably won't take more than a day or two. If it is the couple, the job will go on."

"Here's what they look like." Driscoll pushed another photograph my way, this one of a man and woman about the age of my mother and dad. "We were able to rent a house across the street, 275 Willow. Not directly across, we didn't get that lucky, but close enough for surveillance. It's a shabby two-bedroom built back in the twenties, much like the one we'll be watching, except that one is gray and ours a dingy yellow. Now, here's the wrinkle, Grace. We'll be staying in the house together, you and I."

Both men waited for a reaction. Frankly, the whole thing was a lot to absorb in two minutes so all I did was nod. My heart picked up speed but they couldn't see that.

"I'll leave for work in the morning like normal, you'll stay there all day to watch, but we'll both be there at night." Driscoll stared at me, drumming his fingers on the table. "So, what's your decision, Grace? In or out?"

"I'm in!"

"You're okay with the two of us staying in that house together?"

"I don't know, I guess so."

"I'd take her tepid reaction as an insult, Driscoll, if I were you," Bobby said with a grin.

"But, it's part of the job. Right?" I said.

"Only teasing, Grace. Of course, it's part of the job."

"Purely professional, part of the cover," Driscoll added.

Said that way, it did not seem so improper to spend the night alone with Driscoll. There was something sad about that.

"We start on Sunday. It'll take Bobby and me that long to get the place set up. We arranged for a private telephone line and we're in the process of furnishing it with basics. It's always best to tell as few lies as possible, Grace, but for this one we'll need to tell quite a few. My cover name is Ray Appleman, I just rented that house and I work for Piedmont Petro."

"The company next door?"

"Yeah. I can use the Petro door to come and go, and they'll tell me if anybody inquires. We do little jobs for them and they provide us with occasional cover. We have a car for times like this, too, a clean car registered to Ray Appleman. You are my sister, Grace Appleman, who wants to be a writer, working on your first novel. Gives you a reason to spend long hours in the house."

"What all did this couple do, if I'm allowed to ask."

"You can ask but I can't answer, at least not yet. There shouldn't be anything dangerous about the job. All you're gonna do is sit there and watch. Between the two of us we need to be at that window from dawn 'til dark. That's fourteen or fifteen hours. I'll do early and late but the major chunk will be yours."

"Boredom will be the greatest threat," Bobby said.

"What should I tell them at the boarding house? About where I'm going, I mean."

Driscoll thought a moment. "Tell Maudie the truth but don't say anything to the others. If they ask, Maudie can tell them you're visiting your roommate at school. Remember, we don't lie any more than necessary. Other questions?" Driscoll pushed away from the table.

"You probably can't answer any of them."

"Probably not. Go back home, throw a suitcase together, and work on a title and description for your novel, in case somebody asks."

Sixteen

Driscoll arrived after breakfast Sunday morning, grabbed my suitcase and carried it out to the trunk of the clean car, a dark green Hudson.

"Ham biscuits from Maudie," I said, placing a paper bag between us on the seat. "Have you seen anybody at the house yet?"

"Nobody, not even a vehicle. It looks deserted. I met the man next door. He's a guard at the county jail, lives alone except for a fierce German Shepherd, also a guard at the jail. I gave him our cover story."

Shabby was a good word for the houses on Willow Drive, like Driscoll said. However, rows of sprawling shade trees raised the neighborhood a bit. Matter of fact, with all those lovely oaks and maples it should have been a pleasant place to live, but for me that day, imagination working overtime, it gave off an eerie kind of quality because of that house across the street.

"I wonder what could be going on over there to interest the Central Intelligence Agency," I said.

"Now is not the time to figure it out," Driscoll warned as he parked at the curb. "You're not supposed to be interested in that house, so just turn your head toward ours." As we got out, a man with a dog approached us. "Here's that neighbor I told you about."

The man shook hands with Driscoll and nodded at me. "You must be Grace. I'm Glen Eldon, right next door. I work four to midnight, home most of the day, so stop in if you need a cup of something." He rested a hand on the animal's head. "This is Elsa."

"Is she friendly? Is it okay to pet her?" I held out my hand.

"Easy girl," Glen said, pulling tight on the lead. "Maybe later, after she gets to know you."

"But there won't be such a thing as *later* will there?" I whispered to Driscoll on the way up the sidewalk. "We'll just disappear one day as quick as we came, and he'll never know why. Seems a shame, doesn't it?" Driscoll glanced down at me and didn't say anything. "Do you think it's good or bad to have an armed guard and his dog next door?"

"Doesn't matter so much to us, but I wonder about the folks over there."

Our rental had four cement steps to the porch, wheat-colored siding that probably started out yellow, and a green front door. Driscoll used a key to open it. "We'll leave this locked at all times, day and night. Same with the door in the kitchen that dumps out to the back yard."

Living room and kitchen could be seen from where we stood, plus stairs leading up to the bedrooms. The living room was out of the ordinary. Driscoll's camera with the giant lens sat on a tripod in front of a picture window covered over with curtains that looked to me like a complicated spider web. Two kitchen chairs pulled up close with a small table between.

Behind them, in the center of the room, a pair of comfortable chairs, the upholstered kind, with another little table.

I handed him the bag from Maudie. He fished out a biscuit and ate while he talked. "We put up these sheer curtains last night. The loose weave works well for this sort of thing. You can take a good picture by aiming right through one of the larger holes. Nobody will see us in here unless they're standing in the flower bed, except at night when the lights are on."

"But, will we turn them on?"

"Sure, we will. That's what regular people do and we want to act regular. The camera will be useless after dark, anyway, so we'll just slide it back from the window and shift ourselves to the armchairs. That'll be our nighttime position. We can read from there or listen to a program on the radio I brought in."

Driscoll took my suitcase and carried it up the stairs. I followed. "Your room is this one on the right, bathroom at the end of the hall." I saw how it was up there. He'd put himself in the front bedroom and me in the back. Both rooms had a bed and night table. That was all, except for a lamp and one of those big floor fans.

We did not stay long from the job. Downstairs again, Driscoll motioned me into a kitchen chair and gave a quick camera lesson. "Okay, now play with it a little bit and get comfortable with the zoom. We need to keep a log of what happens—when they come and go, who visits them and for how long. That's what this notebook is for." He nodded at the one on the table.

I did what he said, practiced peering into the camera and got a feel for close-ups. They were really quite remarkable. I could see the paint peeling off the shutters and the dry, brown edges on a bush needing water. I zoomed in on the front porch and out, in again to the sidewalk, followed it to the street and over to our car. Then I widened the view to everything and just left it that way.

The house seemed deserted, like Driscoll said. No car out front but there were blackish stains (probably car oil) on the street by the curb. I sat in the chair and watched for an hour, ready to pounce on the camera at the first sign of … well, anything.

"I hope you like TV dinners," he called from the kitchen.

We kept watch while we ate, and on until dark. After that we moved away from the windows to the upholstered chairs, and with the lights on like normal, we listened to *Gunsmoke* and *Frontier Gentleman*. Driscoll had his head in the Sunday news at the same time. I paid only half attention myself, feeling awkward twinges about those bedrooms and spending the night.

At ten o'clock I announced with a yawn, "Guess I'll say goodnight and go up."

Driscoll had switched to the funny papers by then. He glanced at me and politely nodded, then turned the page and let out a chuckle, probably over his favorite, *Moon Mullins*.

Well, if he could be that casual about it, so could I.

Monday morning, before daybreak, I heard sounds of him in the shower and felt like I shouldn't listen. Actually, I didn't hear much because of the wonderful fan, which was doing a fine job of sucking cool air in from the open window and blowing it around. I lay there and smiled into the darkness for a minute or two, then kicked off the covers and leaped out of bed remembering what had to be done—bathe, dress, make the bed, see about breakfast—all before taking up watch.

When Driscoll came out and then closed his bedroom door, I slipped into the hall in a robe and took my turn in the bathroom.

Downstairs a half hour later, I found him staring out the living room window. He had already moved the camera into the daytime position. "That car came in last night. Had to be sometime after one because I sat in the dark and watched until then. Look. A black Desoto in need of a wash, about as inconspicuous as you can get. Just the type a fugitive would pick."

"That's a Virginia license plate," I said.

"Yes, I just called it in."

"Called it in to whom?"

"Our contacts."

"Our CIA contacts?"

"Yes, Grace, our CIA contacts," he said, chuckling. "Take some good shots of it when you finish that." He nodded at the toast in my hand. "You should be able to find lunch from the groceries I brought. You like sandwiches, don't you?" He touched my shoulder and gave it a squeeze. "Call if you need me. I'll be back around five."

Watching him take long strides down the sidewalk, I could still feel the warmth of his hand and liked it far too much. I set my toast on the table to get the car and license plate on film, my interest growing larger by the minute about that house. At least now we knew somebody was in there. And whoever they were, it was CIA who cared, CIA waiting to hear. Not only that, Driscoll said *our* contacts, which I took to include me.

I sat in the kitchen chair and watched all morning. Saw Glen walking his dog and zoomed in to try him on for size. Hair cut short, not very tall, body like a weightlifter. The age seemed right (I put him at early twenties).

At noon I ran to the bathroom and back, grateful to find the dusty Desoto still there. For lunch, I quickly smeared peanut butter on a banana and chased it down with an icy Coca-Cola. Other than a trip to the bathroom in the afternoon, and an occasional pace in front of the window, I sat there all day.

Driscoll found me like he'd left me. He walked in carrying a newspaper and a white paper bag. "Hamburgers from White Tower," he said, before I could ask. "Smell good?"

"Sure does. I'm starved."

Like the evening before, we watched the window during dinner and kept it up until dark, then moved to our nighttime position, turned on the table lamp and the radio. This time, *Amateur Hour*. I love that show.

On Tuesday I sat and watched all morning, same as the day before. Noon found me hurrying to the bathroom and back. Then, a quick trip to the kitchen for bread, cheese, mayonnaise and a knife—the makings of lunch. Back at my spot, I built myself a sandwich and ate it right there.

Except for the bathroom again, I just stared out the window all afternoon. Got sleepy once and fought it off, remembered Bobby calling boredom the greatest threat.

At that point I could have reported to our contacts that the sidewalk had seventeen cracks with dandelions poking out, the house had six shutters across the front, each with seven slats for a total of forty-two. And the house, up close, did not appear gray at all, but more like a dirty white. A pale blue curtain, one I could not see through, covered their picture window. Two windows upstairs, both with shades cracked and pulled down. Probably in a bedroom. Driscoll had two windows in his bedroom and their house was likely the same.

As for the car, there were countless scratches on the side I could see, a hubcap missing, and a dented back fender.

At five o'clock, two things happened. Driscoll pulled up around the same time that a man and woman finally made an appearance over there! I didn't notice them at first, focused as I was on Driscoll. They were halfway down the sidewalk before I started with the camera.

Driscoll turned to them and the two men shook hands. Then the three stood in the street to talk. I took close-ups the entire time, including some of Driscoll wearing a smile. I got better photos of the license plate as the couple pulled away.

Driscoll used his key to unlock the front door and came to stand behind me. "Did you get some decent shots?"

"Certainly hope so, because I think it's them."

"I'm sure of it."

"With you there, I'm surprised they came out of the house."

"Curious, is my guess. No reason to suspect people who were already here, but we just moved in and they've learned to be suspicious."

"What all did you talk about?"

"Oh, the usual stuff. They introduced themselves as the Gambrells. I gave them our cover story. You might run into them on the street like I just did, so be prepared to answer questions about that novel you're writing. They were quite curious about us. I gave them as little information as possible but they play the same game better. Especially the woman, trying to get more than she gives. That's the one to watch. She's the brains behind whatever they're up to. Mark my words."

Driscoll unloaded the camera and held up the roll of film. "These photographs will tell the tale one way or another, so we need quick turnaround here. Can you reload this thing?" he asked with a hand on the camera. I nodded.

Then, he left the house with the film in his pocket, without any dinner. And he didn't get back until late.

Seventeen

Wednesday morning, Glen Eldon came out to walk his dog. Nothing unusual about that, but on the way back he swerved onto our sidewalk and ended up knocking on the door. It was an unexpected visit, or maybe it wasn't. In the few seconds given me to decide, it seemed right to answer but wrong to let him in the house.

So, I simply stepped out on the porch and it worked just fine. Tricky business, though, remembering to be Grace Appleman instead of myself and to watch across the street the whole time. It got easier once I started him talking about Roanoke and his job at the jail. I could tell he was interested in me, which was nice. Then, Elsa went so far as to sniff my held-out hand and let me rub her on the head. It was fun while it lasted but being so far from the camera seemed a bad idea. I cut the visit short and told myself to discuss with Driscoll the entire notion of people stopping in. What if the others tried it?

The rest of the morning could be described as humdrum, but by the afternoon I was loving the job! If you assume, dear reader, that the couple across the street was the right couple, you'd be correct. I mean, why else would I be telling you all this? Our photographs proved it. They were the missing couple using assumed names, Jim and Betty Gambrell.

After dark, Driscoll brought in equipment hidden under a tarp and carried it upstairs to the front bedroom. I followed and watched him uncover it. "Hey, that's a movie camera!" It was a complicated-looking thing attached to a heavy wood tripod. I had seen ones like this before, in the hands of reporters outside courthouses, including Salem after Stewart Osten's arraignment.

Driscoll placed a hand on the camera with what appeared to be great affection. "Yes, this is a 16-millimeter movie camera," he said as though introducing it to me. "But it's been modified to take time-lapsed still shots. We invested in it for a job last October and it's just what we need for this twenty-four-hour watch. We're entering into the second phase, which permits us to know more. The Gambrells apparently fled Northern Virginia when their contact, someone working at CIA, got caught removing material, presumably to sell to the Soviets. It was classified material, critical to our national defense. They believe the Gambrells acted as intermediaries."

"Those people are spies?"

"Not just ordinary spies. They're Americans, committing treason."

"And here they are, lying low across the street. But they look so normal. The man reminds me of my high school science teacher."

"The Gambrells work hard to appear normal so they can deceive people like us. It's a profession to them and they do it with skill. CIA intends to arrest the pair but they first hope to use them to snag another spy, a high-level Soviet who entered the United States illegally on a forged passport and the false name, Howell. Here's a photograph of him."

Driscoll slid a glossy 8x10 out of a folder, and a man with pockmarked cheeks stared out with cold, cold eyes. He looked to be from another world, a darker one. Gave me the willys, even in a photograph.

"Howell might already have a relationship with the Gambrells, ready to set them up in a similar scheme. Our contacts are very interested in anyone who visits because, well … it could be him."

"Driscoll, what if they come over and knock on the door?"

"I doubt they'll do that, but if they do you cannot let them in. If they see the set-up here, they'll be gone."

"Then, what should I do? They'll know I'm in here."

"Keep the door locked and don't answer. Better for them to wonder about that than question why you won't invite them in."

"Yeah, and they could force their way around me."

"Nah, these people aren't violent, not the Gambrells, anyway. I doubt they even own a gun. People like that, if they want to get rough with somebody, they hire a professional."

"Is that supposed to make me feel better?"

"You worried? What happened to that fearless young coed I first met?"

"She's hiding under the bed. And, Driscoll, what if Glen comes over and knocks on the door?"

He blinked at me. "You'll need to step out on the porch to talk to him. Wouldn't you do that anyway rather than invite a man in when you're alone?"

"Actually, he did come over this morning and that's just what I did."

"What did he want?"

"Nothing. Just to visit, I guess. Elsa warmed up enough to sniff my hand."

Driscoll turned from the topic and positioned the movie camera about three feet from the window, then played with it to get a good view of the sidewalk and front door across the way.

"You won't need to touch this camera, Grace. I'll reload every morning and it will take still shots every ten seconds, around the clock. The problem with it is the limited detail. It'll merely serve as backup during the day. We still need the zoom shots, dawn until dark."

All during Thursday I sat in my chair and watched. It made me wonder about the Gambrells, what the pair of them did in that house all day, whether they were always on their guard. Were they watching us the same as we were watching them?

In the misty light of Friday morning, I found Driscoll down there standing by the window.

"Anything going on?" I asked from the kitchen.

"A rogue squirrel chased a cat up a tree. Does that count?"

I walked in carrying a bowl of cereal and a banana. "Gosh, the squirrels in Betula never do that."

With a touch of sparkle in his eyes, Driscoll seemed to smile at the sight of me. He put a hand on my shoulder as I sat down by the camera. "Well, I'm off. Call to report anything that happens."

"Driscoll, you don't need to tell me that every morning. Of course, I'll call if something happens."

He laughed at that as he went out the door with Thursday's movie reel hidden in a paper bag under an arm.

Glen stopped by again around eleven. I stepped out on the porch with a cracker in my pocket. He let me feed it to Elsa, who nudged my hand for more. "Want to take in a movie this weekend?" he asked. "I'm off on weekends so anytime is fine."

This pleased me and I wasn't surprised. After a pause I gave the only possible answer. "That would be nice, Glen, but I can't right now. Another time, maybe."

He nodded, obviously disappointed.

It was a truthful answer—that would be nice, but I can't. And maybe we *could* go another time, when this was all over. I needed to get my mind off Driscoll somehow.

The sky turned gray and the temperature dropped as we stood out there. After lunch it started to rain.

Around 2:30 in the afternoon, somebody raised the shade on an upstairs window, the one on the right. Now, that was a first. I thought it might mean something, some kind of sign, so I told Driscoll.

A half-hour later, a man came into view walking on the street in a raincoat, black umbrella over his head. There was no identifying him, not with that umbrella, not even zooming in. But, sometimes you just know things and, from my prickly willy symptoms, I knew it was the Soviet spy.

I took a picture, recorded the time in the notebook, and watched with only the eyes in my head as he turned and headed up the Gambrell's sidewalk.

Aiming the camera on the front door, I got a shot of Jim Gambrell opening it.

The visitor trudged up the steps, closed his umbrella and leaned it against the house. That's when I got a decent shot of his face. Only a profile, though, and with a hat.

I reported it to Driscoll. "The man was on foot so he must have a car parked somewhere."

According to Bobby, there weren't many places nearby for a car to sit. The best bet was a church parking lot a quarter-mile away. He was going to put himself there to watch.

All tensed up, I sat in my chair and wore out my gum waiting for the guy to leave. He stayed in there over an hour. When the front door finally opened and he stepped out, I got one full-faced, pockmarked shot before he turned to reach for the umbrella.

With the hat pulled low, collar turned high, and umbrella over his head, he was trying to hide. But, it was Howell. It gave me the shivers watching him plod along the wet sidewalk and disappear down the street.

A few minutes later, comparing times, Bobby saw a man get into a Packard and drive away. Using the pictures we both took, our contacts confirmed it was Howell.

The window shade stayed up all evening but somebody pulled it down before dawn the next day. We all believed it had been a sign, an "all clear" sign to the man.

"We need to assume it wasn't coincidence," Driscoll said. "Can't afford the time to prove it with another test. When that shade goes up again we'll send out a warning immediately. And the same thing the moment we spot Howell on the street. We'll instigate a raid on the house while we have the chance."

Instigate a raid on the house! Boy, I loved this job! Frankly, I wanted to abandon the entire idea of college and just stay undercover.

Eighteen

Saturday morning, Driscoll stayed home. I was the one who left the house and drove to the store to get something for dinner. Ran into Glen and Elsa on the street when I returned.

Elsa sniffed at the bag of groceries Glen had taken out of my hands. "I've got Fig Newtons in there," I said. "Can she have one?"

"Depends. How about her owner? Can he have one, too?"

"We'll all have one."

Glen set the bag on a porch step for me to reach in. I dug around the meat and vegetables for the pack of cookies, tore it open and took four. Elsa got hers first and wolfed it down, alert for another.

I gave two to Glen. "Can Elsa have this last one?" I asked, holding it out.

He nodded, latched onto my hand and suggested a movie again. This forced me to refuse again without giving a reason, when all I wanted to do was explain.

Driscoll met me at the door and took the bag. "What was that about?"

"Fig Newtons."

"Fig Newtons?"

"Yeah, I gave some to Glen and Elsa. She was interested in our groceries and I couldn't very well give her the steak."

Driscoll set the bag on the counter in the kitchen.

"Glen asked me to a movie again."

"Again?"

"He asked the same thing yesterday. Guess I forgot to mention it."

"What did you say?"

"Why, I turned him down, of course. What else would I do in the circumstances?"

"Do you want to go?"

"To a movie? I'd love a movie. You can count on one hand the ones I've seen and still have fingers left."

"But, do you want to go with him?"

"Nah, it would be too complicated, pretending all the while to be somebody else."

"What if the circumstances were different? What then?"

"I still wouldn't want to go," I said automatically. What I really wanted to say was, 'why don't you take me?' but being the woman as well as the younger, I couldn't do that. I mean, what if he didn't want to take me. What if he frowned at the very idea. Or worse, what if he laughed.

Truth was, he was already frowning. It looked like anger to me. No, actually, on further study, it looked like a jealous frown.

We spent the rest of the morning and all afternoon in that little house, watching out the window together. Not one thing happened, at least not out there, but plenty went on inside between Driscoll and me.

It was subtle stuff. Resting a hand on my shoulder, he let it linger. Adjusting the camera, he crowded my space. He came

132

up with all sorts of reasons to put his hands on me. Nothing improper, nothing like that. Subtle stuff on one hand but, all added up, the path it took seemed huge. Maybe I was making too much of it. After all, most of it could have gone on between any two friends. Except, I saw desire in his eyes and it wasn't about Fig Newtons.

Near dinner time while Driscoll kept watch, I set potatoes in to bake. When they were almost done, while I kept watch, Driscoll put steaks in to broil.

We ate our fine meal on paper plates and talked about subjects we hadn't covered before. Our broken romances, for one. I shared painful truths about my breakup with Obie. He told me about an Italian girl—a beautiful, long-haired Italian girl, is what he said. It was my turn to be jealous, hearing him talk that way.

He'd fallen in love with her in Europe, wanted to bring her to America as a bride but she did not want to leave mom and dad. I got up the nerve to ask if he'd gone all the way with her, or anybody else.

First, he looked surprised at such a bold question, but he got over it quick and fired back a mature, shameless yes.

What a silly thing to ask. A man of twenty-eight? Of course, he had. Maybe there's something peculiar about me, but I was not bothered by that answer. The way I see it, experience in these matters is a good thing in a man, as long as he did not cheat on me to get it.

As for my experience, Driscoll merely raised a questioning eyebrow, too much of a gentleman to ask. I gave him a serious shake of the head, followed by, "nope, uncharted territory for me," which was completely true if you didn't count necking.

Later, up in my room, I stared out at the night and felt something stirring between Driscoll and me, a kind of heat.

On Sunday morning I returned to the boarding house for some different clothes. By design, I got there in time for breakfast, found Maudie in the kitchen spooning oatmeal into bowls from a copper pot, her mouth pooched out in concentration. I stood there and watched.

"You've got something on your mind. What is it?" she asked.

"I'd like to be older."

She stopped spooning and turned to me. "Well, I'd like to be younger, but here we are."

"It's just that, do you think two people can be suited to each other even with a big age difference?"

"In general, or do you have certain people in mind?"

"Just in general."

"Uh-huh." She aimed a look of disbelief at me. "Well, that's a subject for later. Right now, you can help put this food on the table. I warned the colonel about the abbreviated menu. Clarisse is sleeping in and I didn't expect you, so it was only to be the three of us for oatmeal, eggs and cinnamon toast."

Surprisingly, the colonel had nothing to say on the subject of biscuits, too worked up over current events the rest of us apparently missed. He stabbed his fork at each of us. "I just don't understand today's military leaders."

"What have they done now, Colonel?" Maudie asked.

"It's what they haven't done. The fighting in Korea ended in late July, an armistice signed to create a 'no military' zone between the north and south."

"Isn't that good?"

"Yes, yes, it's good, but they haven't signed a peace treaty yet. That's the point I'm trying to make. Until they do they're still at war, and that is bad."

He held the bowl of oatmeal up to his mouth, took a heaping bite and swallowed without chewing.

"And another thing … the United States returned almost four hundred ships to West Germany, ships we captured during the war. That's okay for now, Chancellor Adenauer is on our side. But what about the next chancellor? What about later? Those ships could be firing at us again."

My mind started to wander. Frankly, I didn't much care about Germany or Korea. At that moment, the Soviet Union seemed the greater threat. The colonel carried on like that the entire meal but at least nobody asked where I had been, which spared me from telling lies.

After breakfast, Maudie and I cleared the table, stacked dishes on the kitchen counter beside the sink. I pulled a clean towel out of a drawer. Maudie soaped up a dish, dunked it in rinse water, handed it to me to dry. And we went on that way.

"Now, about big age differences," she said. "I know only one thing, but I know it for sure. It works just fine if the man is older, in case you're thinking of a situation like that. Never works the other way around. A woman's appearance is naturally more important than a man's and, before long, she'll get to worrying about being the older and it won't matter if she doesn't look it. She'll start to doubt herself and then doubt him, assume he feels trapped and out to find somebody younger. Then she'll turn jealous and accusing until she drives the man away."

"Gosh, you seem to know a lot about it."

"Not from my experience, no. I was three months younger than George and he got killed before either of us could see old. No, it's what happened to Miss Scott, I'm referring to."

"Our Miss Scott?" I asked, nodding toward the dining room.

135

"The very same. Married a man thirteen years younger during the war, one of those quick weekend courtships. She was already forty-two but quite attractive back then."

"Don't you think she's still attractive?"

"Yes, but she was *very* attractive ten years ago. A traffic stopper, you might say. He was a full-of-energy master sergeant named Jones. Don't recall his first name. A good man, and mad about her. It could have worked out fine. But after the war she looked in the mirror and worried about all those younger women without a man. Her jealousy drove him right out the door to find one. It ended in divorce. He's remarried with two kids. She switched back to her maiden name and moved in here, living on the money he paid just to escape her. It's been nice for me, though, the steady income. She's clean and quiet, and I like her company, now that she has mellowed."

I picked up a clean stack of dishes and set them in the cupboard.

"This is about Driscoll, I presume. Has anything happened between you?" She asked the question but didn't wait for an answer. "Well, the man's a dream, is all I can say. He's honest. He enjoys my cooking and lets me know it. And, he's clean. Any woman would be lucky to get him. And there's nothing wrong with you being younger," she said, giving me a squeeze.

I spent most of the day with Maudie, back to her cooking and the chance to do something besides watch out a window. By Sunday evening, though, I was eager to get my stuff together and leave. Maudie packed up leftover dinner for Driscoll and gave it to me at the door.

Nineteen

On Monday morning, Driscoll walked out of the house in the usual routine, left me alone to stare out the window and daydream about him.

Just before lunch, the front door opened over there. A moment later Betty Gambrell broke out and skipped down the porch steps. Going to the store, I figured, except she didn't have a purse. Before I could think how odd that was, she was at the end of the sidewalk and stepping into the street. She was headed right to me!

Driscoll said it wouldn't happen! I jumped up, told myself not to panic, quickly slid the camera into the night position. By this time she was approaching the porch steps. Seconds later, a knock on the door. I hugged the wall and held my breath. She knocked again and waited. Then she leaned on the doorbell. I could feel her impatience and hoped she did not have a talent for picking locks.

The telephone rang. Had to be Driscoll. I let it ring.

She went back down the steps, stopped in front of the house and looked toward the window, shielding her eyes from the sun's glare. I watched from a safe distance, grateful for the flower bed.

All at once it hit me. If they were suspicious of newcomers, wouldn't *not* answering make it worse? On impulse I yanked open the door and ran out on the porch.

"Hello, excuse me! I'm here," I said with a wave. She turned around to look. I picked up my pace to get away from the house as she headed back to me. "Sorry for not answering. I was working upstairs."

"Just wondered if you had any cream."

If that was an excuse, it was flimsy. "Gosh, sorry, I'm afraid we don't." It was a lie, but a necessary one. Giving her any cream would have meant going into the house.

"Oh, that's okay. I'll get to the store later. Your brother said you're a writer."

"Well, trying to be."

"What are you working on?"

"A novel, my first." I said this with a shy tilt to the head, getting into the act.

"I always wanted to do that. What's it called?"

"Mountain Justice."

"Hmm, interesting title. What's it about?"

"Well, it takes place in a small town that likes things peaceful. Anyone who messes with it tends to disappear."

"A fictional town?"

"Oh yeah, it's all pure fiction." Another lie. Truth was, I could write such a book as a true account.

"You said you were working upstairs. My, isn't it hot on the second floor?"

"I'm in the back bedroom. It's actually better up there. The sun's so hot in the front of the house, and we have big fans in the bedrooms. You know, for sleeping."

"Just the opposite for us. Hotter in the back, cooler in the front."

She said she wanted to read my novel sometime, and I said she could. Nothing more interesting than that. I figured it was just the sort of meaningless talk to take suspicions away.

When Driscoll got home he called it smart, what I did. Besides, it was already done. He supported the lie about the cream and said I was right to tell him. Details like that, handled badly, could blow a cover, he said.

The next few days, I watched and hoped for another sign with the window shade. Unrealistic to expect it so soon, though. I mean, how often would this spy visit? Every time Howell surfaced he was taking a real chance.

Driscoll said we just needed to keep calm and stay the course, take note of their suspicious activities without doing anything suspicious ourselves.

Now, that was funny. If the couple over there saw all the necking over here, our brother-sister story would've been blown for sure.

It began innocently enough. He'd been touching my shoulders a lot already, which turned into massage as I sat at the window trying to watch. From that, he formed a steady habit of scratching my back. Then, little by little, his hands drifted lower until they were giving my waist a nice rub.

Maybe I should've stopped him at that point but I just didn't want to. Like a dozen daydreams, his hands moved around to the sides and then stretched to the front, wrapping the whole of my waist in his grip. My waist has always been sensitive to a man's touch and he soon reached the limit of what I could take without reacting.

I popped out of the chair, turned to face him, and that was that. We crossed the line from business to personal, a one-way trip. It was so unprofessional and risky. We both knew it. If a busload of Russian spies dressed in red had chosen then to appear, we wouldn't have noticed.

Over a dinner neither of us ate, we had a talk and promised to cool down. I decided, being the woman, that it was mostly my job to stay away from him. But it wasn't easy. Truth was, I had it bad for Driscoll. I'd seen another side—the manly, physical, aggressive side. And when you mix that with the Driscoll I already knew—aloof, serious, and polite to a fault, well …

Once we had crossed that line, staying in the house together at night felt suddenly wrong, but there was nothing to be done. Driscoll said we just needed to buck up and be professional. It was part of the job. We both understood without saying anything that we were completely off-limits to each other on the second floor.

The next few days, the daytimes were easy with him being gone, but neither of us did such a good job when he got home.

For instance on Thursday evening, still in our daytime positions, he pulled me back from the window, hooked me in his arms and we soon got pretty steamed up. In an attempt to save us both from a mistake, I finally pulled away to catch my breath and smooth my hair. He stepped back as well, sat on the arm of an upholstered chair and took a deep breath. "Grace," he said with his serious voice, "before this goes any further, we need to talk about the viability of a future together. Probably should have done it a month ago."

"The viability?"

"I'm referring to our age difference, whether we're too far apart."

"Maudie says age difference is not an issue at all if the man is the older one."

"She did? You've discussed this with her?"

"Well, yes."

"I guess that's good, but how do *you* feel? Don't you mind that I'm nine years older?"

"No, I like that you're older. Don't you mind that I'm nine years younger?"

"Why should I mind? All the advantage is on my side—a man my age with a beautiful college girl."

"Gosh, Driscoll, is that really how you see me?"

"Of course, it is." He pulled me close again, kissed both sides of my face and rubbed my back, trying not to start up again.

"What if I weren't a college girl?" I asked with my lips against his cheek.

"What do you mean?"

I leaned back to look at his face. "I mean, would you be disappointed if a I weren't a college girl?"

"Of course not. After all, you won't always be a college girl."

"I'm talking about now, Driscoll. Truth is, I don't want to go back to college. Can't I just stay here and work with you?"

"Now, wait a minute, you can't make a decision like that in the heat of emotion. And not every job is as exciting as this, or even the one at the post office."

That night I was robbed of my sleep analyzing what all happened between Driscoll and me, what got said and what didn't. He had yet to speak of love. Obie had never spoken of love either, not to me, anyway. With my mouth empty of gum, I chewed on that awhile and came to one conclusion: I needed Driscoll to say the words.

On Friday morning, as he left the house, it was all strictly business again, both of us focused on what could happen across the street. Howell had come on Friday the week before. Maybe it was a Friday thing. I was to telephone Driscoll immediately about window-shade activity or any activity over there.

But at five o'clock, still waiting, he hurried home.

"Do you think we might have spooked the couple somehow?" I asked. "Maybe they're watching us with some high-powered camera of their own."

"But we know they're not. If they could see in here, they'd already be gone."

Twenty

Saturday morning we weren't interested in eating. Living on love, I guess. We watched out the window together, touching hands, until around nine-thirty when Driscoll got ready to leave. "I hate to cut out on you like this but time marches on. We need to meet a client about another job."

"Another undercover job?"

"Well, yes, it'll probably come to that."

"Anything fit for me?"

"Not unless you're experienced as a machine operator or forklift driver. Are you? It wouldn't surprise me." He grinned and gave me a brotherly kiss on the cheek. "It's for a tool company with labor problems. Bobby will go in if need be. He knows enough to fake it."

Driscoll put the previous night's reel in a bag and stuck it under an arm. "Call me about anything, just anything at all."

Yeah, yeah, yeah. I watched his car go out of sight and then sat there dreaming about the future, the two of us undercover together in all sorts of jobs.

Half an hour into it, the window shade went up.

Driscoll stopped to take my call, his meeting barely started. "I'll warn the people up the line. This could be it," he said.

I suddenly felt a need to eat. Not from hunger, exactly, more for nerves. A quick run to the kitchen would have been lovely, for cereal or cinnamon toast, but nothing was worth missing that first glimpse of Howell.

I picked through a basket of snacks on the table, devoured peanut butter crackers and a freckled banana. Ten minutes later or maybe less, I opened a pack of Twinkies, ate one and washed it down with a lukewarm Coca-Cola. I had just bitten into the other Twinkie when Howell appeared on the street, in the opposite direction from the time before. I quickly called Driscoll.

"On my way, Gracie," he said. "Stay inside and expect a crowd."

The Gambrells were obviously expecting Howell. The door opened over there without a knock and then closed in a rush. He was in there only about ten minutes when Driscoll raced up and parked out front, followed by six more cars that must have been gathering nearby. No sirens, but the speed and screeching tires alone were jarring as cuss words in church. Curious neighbors opened doors, and I bet the three in that house heard all the commotion and knew they were dead ducks.

Driscoll came in to watch with me and we counted fifteen men piling out of the cars. Some broke in the front and others circled around outside.

Almost immediately, the fugitives were led quietly out the door one at a time and down the sidewalk in handcuffs. That was it. So little ceremony, so little fuss. Yet watching it made my hair bristle. Why? Because just before Betty Gambrell turned to climb in the car, she glared across the road at us with icy hatred.

"Well," Driscoll said, "if looks could kill, we'd both be on the floor."

Hearing him say that, I retreated into the fold of his arms out of fear, surprising the both of us.

"Easy, my girl, easy. Don't you worry. They can't hurt anybody. Where they're going, thanks to us, they'll never breath fresh air again or see more than a flash of sky." He kissed my cheek. "Yeah, looks like they figured us out at the eleventh hour. The way I rushed in with the others was a clear sign we were involved."

Bobby soon showed up and joined us in the watch. Outside the house, two men emptied the contents of metal trash cans into paper bags. Others collected evidence inside and carried it out in boxes. Soon, it was all loaded up and hauled away, the house securely locked and marked with a *No Trespassing* sign. Driscoll said others would come later, for fingerprints and such.

After that sudden end, there was nothing to do on our side of the street but pack up and move out. Driscoll and Bobby wrapped the movie camera in the tarp and carried it down the stairs.

"Did anything useful come from that?" I asked.

Driscoll said, "It showed that nothing much happened over there at night. And, the continuous shots will be more helpful than stills to the people building a case."

They packed up the other equipment, took it all outside and loaded it into Bobby's car, discussing that next job all the while. The idea seemed to be for Driscoll to leave with Bobby and continue the meeting while I finish there and follow in the other car. Okay with me. They seemed ready to move on. I needed time to adjust.

In slow motion I packed up the stuff in my bedroom and carried it downstairs. Then I fiddled around in the kitchen, relieving cabinets and the refrigerator of what little food we had left.

The telephone rang. It had to be Driscoll. "You're still there, huh?" he asked.

"Well, yeah, I'm just finishing in the kitchen. Do you need me for something? Is there a rush?"

"No. Frankly, I just wanted to hear your voice."

"Aw, Driscoll, that's sweet. And I don't mind a bit hearing yours."

"I guess it's quiet over there now."

I stood near the window as far as the telephone cord would stretch. "Yeah, just like all the other days we spent looking out. Right now, I'm watching Glen leave."

"To walk Elsa?"

"No, in his car, probably going to the store. He does that on Saturdays."

"Business as usual, then."

As Glen's car disappeared, a man entered my line of sight. I interrupted Driscoll and told him. "A man on the street in the middle of the afternoon, a man in a suit. The only time we saw that was when … if he turns into that sidewalk over there, I'll —"

"What does he look like? Have you seen him before?"

"No, never. Tall and thin, dark hair, coming from the right. Wait a minute … uh, looks like he's heading to *our* house."

"Gracie?"

"He's coming up the sidewalk! I don't like this, Driscoll. Doesn't feel right."

146

"Okay, calm down. Does he have some sort of case? Maybe he's selling something."

I slammed myself against the wall and clung to the telephone, strangely unable to speak and move at the same time.

"Grace, talk to me. Move far away from the window and don't hang up."

I took a deep breath and held it. Maybe the man *was* selling something. I didn't dare look. I heard him come up the steps. He rang the bell. Pause. He rang it again. I expected him to knock. He didn't. He began fiddling with the lock!

"Driscoll, I think he's trying to break in!"

"Get out of there! Now! Out the kitchen door and over to Glen's. I'm calling the police."

I dropped the telephone, broke out the back, got halfway across the lawn. That's when I heard a muffled shot and felt a sharp ping high up on my left arm. Like somebody hit me with a rock. I kept running, made it to Glen's back door and banged on it.

Elsa whined on the other side.

I turned the knob, tumbled in, slammed the door and locked it. Thought about letting the dog loose on the man but knew she'd be shot. Then, remembering the front door, I ran and locked it, too.

By that time, Elsa had turned crazy, attacking the back door with everything in her. She sounded so vicious! You'd think the man, whoever he was, would give up just from that. But he slipped that lock the same as the other and fought to break in, pushing hard against her.

Suddenly, he *was* in and leading with the gun! I figured the dog was a goner, and then it would be me. But Elsa, with a leap, chomped down on his hand and sent that gun flying! It hit the floor somewhere and went off.

Meantime, without any thought, I picked up a frying pan from the stove, swung it over my head and slammed it down on the man's. I was shocked to see him crumble and figured he would rise. Elsa kept growling and continued to stand guard, not trusting that fall as the end of things, either.

Sirens in the distance. Elsa heard them first.

I had forgotten about my arm. There was blood enough at that point to run down and make a puddle on the floor. I stared at it in dizzy surprise at the notion of being shot. And then, just like that, I left the scene.

Twenty-One

From way down in a well I heard Driscoll call my name again and again. I floated to it. He was bent over me with worry on his face. And a dozen other people, it seemed like, stared down at me and that man, conked out on the floor together in a messy mix of blood, dog hair, and bacon grease from the frying pan.

Glen ran in from his trip to the store and witnessed all this. Then, with a look of shock and wonder, he discovered that he'd had spies living across the street and an undercover operation next door.

After Driscoll helped me up and into a chair, they hauled the man out on a stretcher and loaded him into an ambulance.

"I hope he'll be all right," I said with a twinge of guilt.

"Eh, don't worry about him. All he'll have from this, other than an arrest, is a headache and a big goose egg. I'd say, he deserves much worse."

Driscoll insisted on a second ambulance for me. He wanted another stretcher, too, but he couldn't have his way on everything. I walked out and climbed in on my own. I must have swallowed my gum at some point, or lost it, because it was gone when I went to chew it during the ride. While an attendant fixed my arm with a temporary bandage, the ambulance driver had a lot to say about what happened, most of it flattering to me.

"Well, I can knock a man out with a frying pan, whatever that proves," I said, bringing a laugh. Although, this man had not stood a chance against Elsa and me so, as a hired gun, he must have been a newcomer to the trade.

At the hospital they removed the bullet, patched me up and put me in a bed. I fell asleep. Driscoll arrived sometime later, woke me up with a kiss and folded himself into a chair. "Just so you know, the man wasn't only after you. Bobby and I agree that he was out for the two of us. With the car parked outside he thought we'd both be there." He picked up my hand and sighed. "Oh, Grace, I'm so sorry to put you in danger like this. If anything more serious had happened to you ..."

"But it didn't. This is not the first time I've been shot at, Driscoll, or even the second."

"Yeah, but it was the first time you were hit, and I got you into this one."

They took the gunman straight from the hospital to the county jail wearing hand cuffs and a compress on his noggin. I stayed overnight and left the next day with my bandaged arm in a sling.

It felt good to be back in my own life, the safety of my own name, back to the boarding house for Maudie to make a fuss over me. She knew the truth about my arm but we told the others it had been injured in a clumsy fall.

There were reports on the radio and in the Sunday news about the incidents on Willow Drive. There was talk of it at the dining table, too. Maudie and I just looked at each other.

The next afternoon, Driscoll came for Sunday dinner. I was still up in my room when he arrived. Actually, I was in the bathroom applying makeup, something I had not done all those days at the rental house, not even lipstick.

I think Clarisse was waiting for him. She'd gone downstairs early and must have positioned herself in the parlor, because she was right there to open the door. I heard her greet him with that voice of hers and imagined her hand on his arm or his chest, wherever she'd decided to put it.

What did I do? I skipped down the stairs and rushed right into his arms. He did not kiss me in front of her but he nuzzled my neck, which was almost as good.

Clarisse looked surprised and flustered, put hands on her cheeks that were red as tomatoes, and stepped away. She must have felt like yesterday's oatmeal and I felt a bit sorry for her. I could afford to be charitable. Though nothing was official yet and I didn't have a ring, Driscoll said we needed to talk about our future and that was good enough.

At dinner, I wanted to blurt out everything, but it was too early to talk about Driscoll, and as far as the job, I could never speak of it. Around the table, it was obvious that something had changed between Driscoll and me, which confused everyone but Maudie. The colonel and Miss Scott were too polite to ask questions, and Clarisse just sat there in silence, which was a first as far as I know. At one point I saw her glance at my left hand and then smirk at my naked ring finger. It didn't even bother me.

After dinner, Driscoll and I had the rest of the afternoon for ourselves. He suggested the park. We strolled over there, he found a bench and sat me down, my heart beating double time because he seemed to be setting a scene.

He took my hand, kissed it, and that's when he said he loved me. Completely in love, is what he said. Those words were magic. There was nothing left for me to do but say the same, and I saw no cause to make him wait.

He kissed me at that point, of course. It was the gentlest kiss in the world. I sat there quietly in his arms, my head on his shoulder. Such a tender moment to lock in memory. Then, he removed his arms rather abruptly, straightened his back and turned to me. "Grace, it's time for brutal honesty."

"*Brutal* honesty?"

"About these nine years between us."

"Actually, it's only eight and a half, my birthday being in May and yours in November."

"Okay, but when you turn forty-two, I'll already be fifty. Do you realize that?"

"When you stretch it into the future that way, I think the difference shrinks."

"Then, you really don't mind that I'm that much older? Remember, brutal honesty."

"I thought we already settled this. Driscoll, I've had special feelings for you all summer, even before that, back at school. But I figured you saw me as nothing more than a girl."

He stared at me in surprise. "I stopped viewing you as a girl a long time ago. Frankly, I think arranging your summer job was motivated, at least in part, by my yet-to-be-admitted interest in you. Bobby said it was, anyway."

"You talked to him about it?"

"Oh, yes, at length. Now, it's clear to me that you are everything I want, regardless of your age."

After that little speech, he pulled out a small black box and balanced it on my knee. "Open it," he said, nodding down.

A box that size, it had to be a ring. I took a deep breath and opened it. It was a ring, all right, a diamond, the best in the world! I cried out at the sight of it and fell into his chest with wet eyes.

He was obviously pleased with my reaction because one of his belly laughs slipped out.

Soon, though, I leaned up and stared at him. "Wait a second, is this a proposal?"

"Why, yes, silly goose, of course it's a proposal."

I hesitated. Between Obie and me there'd never been any marriage proposal or acceptance, nothing more than his class ring around my neck and a loose understanding that grew into a plan. We all know how that turned out.

"Do I need to say the words? Is that it? Oh, very well." Driscoll sighed, got down on a knee and said, "Will you marry me, Miss Dawson? Be my adorable, courageous partner for life?"

You gotta admit, that was one fine proposal! I could not imagine a better one and offered my immediate yes.

"You're quite sure?"

"Of course, I'm sure. Especially now that I've seen your passionate side." I said it like a tease.

"Oh? Is that right? Well, good, because I'm afraid you're stuck with it." He looked at me like a meal, wrapped me in his arms and nibbled my neck. We sat there in dreaminess awhile, soaking it all in, until somebody's yappy dog came sniffing and busted us up.

Driscoll removed his arms and studied me. "Now, what's this about not going back to college?"

"Eh, probably a bad idea. I just don't want to leave you, is all."

"Well, something has come up that'll blend in with that."

"What?"

"Another assignment, this one up north in New York."

"With CIA?"

"Yes."

"Just you?"

"Yes."

"How long will you be gone?"

"Hard to say. Several months, I imagine."

"Aw, Driscoll! We just got engaged and you're leaving already. Obie left me for a job and never glanced back."

"Well, I'm not Obie." He kissed his own finger and brought it to my lips. "The way I see it, this won't change much for us. You'll be in school, I'll be in New York, and we'll see each other when we can. Maybe it'll be better this way. I'll pack up my passionate side and take it with me where I can't get my hands on you. And you'll have this ring on your finger, which will tell all the handsome upperclassmen to lay off."

"Now, wait a minute, what about you? Why is it that women don't mark men with engagement rings, too?"

"Beats me. Probably has something to do with money. It's men who do all the spending, you know. Your ring, for example, cost me a whole month's pay."

"Gosh, Driscoll, are you sure you want to do that?" I slid my precious new ring up to the first knuckle. "I can be just as happy with a cheaper one," I said, and mostly meant it.

"I didn't tell you that to brag. Actually, I said it only to prove I'm a saver. Your future husband is a saver, Miss Dawson, and good with money, in case you want to know. I already had the money saved, didn't come anywhere near to draining my bank account. And it was worth every cent just to see your face."

I still hadn't told Driscoll about my inheritance. I opened my mouth to tell him then and decided not to steal his thunder.

"And I'm a planner, too," he went on describing himself.

"Oh? And what will be our plan?"

"A simple one. You have three more years of college. My New York assignment will be over by then. We can marry the day after you graduate."

"Actually, it's almost September, so it's only two years and nine months."

Twenty-Two

Two years and nine months. On this side of the waiting it seems like a long time. It's always been my plan to have a wedding first before all that bedroom business, but Driscoll and I have such short fuses, so I don't know. He's made it easy for me. Even with all the necking, his hands have yet to stray. He deserves credit for that. I had to swat Obie's hands away more than once when they wandered across my chest. Long engagements, short fuses. Who knows how that will play out. But I'll tell you right now, I'm not making any promises.

It'll always be Driscoll for me. Yeah, I said the same thing about Obie, but here's my position on that: We'd still be together if he hadn't walked away. I'm convinced things happen for a reason and this just adds to the evidence. I wasn't supposed to marry Obie in the first place, so a break from him had to happen somehow. I was just a high school girl a year ago, putting all my trust in a high school boy.

It's different with Driscoll. He's already a man who has been to a war and seen what there is of the world. I love that he is older. I love bringing that sparkle to his eyes. I can't make it happen just any old time, so I crave it all the more, want to work at earning it the rest of my life.

K.J. McCall

I know beyond a doubt that we're supposed to be together. Sometimes, you just know things without hearing about them or being told. I mean, we know frogs lay eggs but has anybody ever heard it done?

Last night, Driscoll and I shared a passionate farewell. I'm heading back to Stapleton College and my roommate, Penny Thayer. Penny and I had planned to visit often over the summer. Somehow those plans fell through, but she's already met Driscoll and I know she approves.

Mother insists I invite him home to Betula for Thanksgiving, and his father, too. I know what that's about. Better to have them there with us than me somewhere else. Wouldn't it be amusing if she took to Mr. Driscoll and he took to her. On the other hand, poor man.

Well, there's nothing else to say now so I guess this is goodbye. Except to shine a final light on what just happened here. It's like magic if you think about it: A part of me traveling unhindered by time and distance to meet you, dear reader, in that mystical place where stories take shape.

Maybe we'll meet there again.

Books by K.J. McCall

Set Apart 2010
Eighteen in 1942 2014

Grace Dawson Series 2022
Book 1: Aunt Clara's Secrets
Book 2: The Roommate
Book 3: Other People's Problems